WILLIAM KOTZWINKLE is the author of several acclaimed novels and collections of stories, among which are ELEPHANT BANGS TRAIN, SWIMMER IN THE SECRET SEA, DOCTOR RAT, and FATA MORGANA. His novel THE FAN MAN is now available in an illustrated edition, with drawings by Keith Bendis.

Other Avon books by
William Kotzwinkle

The Fan Man	43125	$4.95
Elephant Bangs Train	38216	2.95
Leopard's Tooth	37382	1.75
Swimmer in the Secret Sea	38646	2.95

NIGHTBOOK

WILLIAM KOTZWINKLE

A BARD BOOK/PUBLISHED BY AVON BOOKS

NIGHTBOOK is an original publication of Avon Books. This work has never before appeared in any form.

AVON BOOKS
A division of
The Hearst Corporation
959 Eighth Avenue
New York, New York 10019

Published by arrangement with the author.
ISBN: 0-380-49106-0

First Equinox Printing, March, 1974.
First Bard Printing, May, 1980

Printed in the U.S.A.

For Elizabeth
With thanks to Fathers:
Herodotus
Plutarch
Homer
Aristophanes
Sophocles
Achilleus Tatios
Ailianos

In order to understand . . . Greek life, we must transport ourselves in thought into a moral latitude totally different from our own.

W. E. H. Lecky
History of European Morals

1

"Did you ever eat a girl?" she asked quietly.

Her legs were well-proportioned and she wore no stockings. The river murmured near, moving through the darkness. He sat on the riverbank beside her on the sand, looking at the lights of the city across the dark body of water.

"No," he said. He was not yet twenty. His car was parked above on the river road. A policeman might see it and wonder, might come down and find them here. Slowly she raised her skirt up over her bare legs.

"Eat me," she said, spreading her legs wide, lifting her body so her crotch hair came out of the shadows of the river trees and glistened in the moonlight.

The river road was not empty. Upon it, traveling by foot, were the most distinguished ladies of Athens, winding their way through the moonlight toward the temple of Demeter. The mystery of the great fertility goddess was being celebrated and to evoke the most potent response it was necessary for these great ladies to attend and participate.

"Eat me," she whispered.

The beautiful Athenians were greeted at the temple doorway by a slave boy, who noted how especially adorned they were this evening, their eyes sparkling, their lips red, their cloaks more immodest and revealing than anything seen in the streets of Athens by day.

Heart pounding, he lowered his head toward the mystery. If the cops find my car, they'll just give it a ticket, that's all.

"Oh, yes, baby," she sighed as his mouth delicately touched her labia, the soft flesh of his mouth sending a thrill of shivering ecstasy through her, up to her belly and down through her thighs.

The High Priestess of Demeter's temple felt a quiver of sweetly subtle joy pass through her body. The Goddess Demeter had entered her, and was now in the temple. The Athenian women gathered together in the main room, seating themselves on lovely cushions of red before a long low banquet table. The Priestess rose from her golden chair and slowly descended the staircase, chatting informally with her beautiful guests. Her own great beauty was matched by a compelling dignity, the inevitable fruit of her renunciation of Athenian society in favor of the hidden company of the Goddess. Yet this evening the Priestess was open and bright, and her casual manner put all the women at their ease, a thing quite rare when so many beauties are gathered under one roof.

The beauty of the Athenian women was lost on the slave boy. His taste was for young men; such is the paradox enjoyed by the gods; the servant of the Fertility Queen was a sodomite. Yet how tempting is the golden thigh of Pythagoras.

"Do you want a drink?" he asked his lover.

"No," replied the pale-faced young man, dressed in a fashionable, immaculately tailored Edwardian suit and sprawled upon a plush red couch in a luxurious Greenwich Village apartment, his eyes closed in review of a dream he'd had recently of walking down a night street. Someone had pointed at him and said, "Thirty-three years old and still a faggot."

Cock. A boy's tanned thighs and the sudden whiteness of his buttocks where his underwear falls away. Hiss. A snake.

The headband of the High Priestess was a serpent, coiled round her forehead, made of gold, with ruby eyes and the cold smile of cold blood, its scales shining with tiny diamonds. She signaled to the slave and a sumptuous meal was served to the distinguished ladies, who ate at the low table in the center of the room, beneath the shadow of the statue of Demeter. They sprawled on cushions, drinking excellent wine. The odor of their perfume was a strong incense offered to Demeter and mingling with it was the still more delicate bouquet of their sex.

Pussy smells good! he realized with joy. The river night was all around him. She said eat me and I'm eating her. He buried his nose deeper into the tangled hairs. You just can't listen to what your friends tell you; it tastes good too. I'm not afraid any more, not of pussy or police.

The slave boy laid one dish after another out for the Athenian women, who toyed with his toga and flirted openly and obscenely—it was the night for such openness but the slave could not respond, filled as he was with fear of these soft creatures. He feared their smell, their taste, their touch, and he feared he would be laughed at if he attempted one of them and failed to produce an erection.

"Thirty-three years old and still a faggot."

"Is it self-analysis time again, my dear?"

"I'm a cocksucker."

"You love it."

The two men looked at each other, one upon the grotesque Victorian couch, the other seated at a round white-marble-topped coffee table. They shared the Greenwich Village apartment, and a neurosis. Their love affair was alternately tempestuous and boring. Once it had been tender, fine, and deep. Now it had grown into a caricature: they'd recently attended a fag costume party, dressed as The Green Cornholer and his faithful chauffeur Cocko. The party had been raided and Cocko and The Green Cornholer had just managed to escape out the window into the waiting Fagmobile, parked on Eighth Street. Two of their friends, who'd come dressed as nuns, had been taken to night court. They'd tried to run, but their long gowns tripped them up and Officer Slug of the vice-squad had made a dazzling arrest.

Fun, yes, but a bit too much. The affair had become jaded. The Green Cornholer stood up from the coffee table. His body was strong, clad in a tight-fitting polo shirt and tight white pants. "I'm going for a walk."

Cocko closed his eyes and remained on the couch. How sad and inevitable it all was that they should love and drift apart. He wanted to go to The Green Cornholer, clasp that strong body in his own, but a heaviness had fallen over his limbs. He could only open his eyes and stare at the ceiling, allowing himself the faint smile of bitterness. "Are you going to be unfaithful again?"

"Perhaps," said The Green Cornholer, and then he was gone through the door and out of the apartment into the night.

Cocko remained on the couch in his elegant pose, limp, with a pure white-lace collar at his neck and lovely curls upon his forehead, staring at the white ceiling in which an old plaster relief mold of a hundred years ago had been restored—round, decorated with flower-shapes and snakes.

The High Priestess smiled and moved her head gently to the gentle music made by her slave upon his lute, and as she moved the eyes of the golden snake upon her forehead seemed to wink at the ladies of Athens, who were finishing their delicious meal. Sipping wine from golden goblets, they had become more relaxed and soon the stories would begin, the rare and obscene love tales told each year by the most beautiful women in the city of beauty—stories of strange lewdness, beloved of Demeter, who would bless them with fruitful wombs.

2

Laying hot and tickled madly in the sand of the river shore, she curled herself like a snake trying to shed an itchy skin, stretching out and pressing deeply into the sand.

Her sex was in his mouth, her legs spread apart. The taste of her was all over his lips and tongue, the smell of her was in his nose, and he pushed his face still deeper into her pubic hair.

The bush parted and the black jungle warriors stepped through, carrying their submachine guns. Their ebony bodies were sleek and powerful in the moonlight. The drums were sounding through the trees. With the warriors was an adolescent boy, his body not yet full, but his time of manhood come. He'd slept alone in the tangled curtain of the jungle night, proving his spirit was strong. Now he must undergo a still more dangerous initiation, for it would free him from the treacherous vines of childhood which wind themselves around a male child at birth and hold him fast. Decked as a warrior, his face and arms brightly painted, he was led to the clearing where fires burned and the old men sat enchanted, squatting beside the dancing flames. He was ushered by the warriors to the hut most familiar to him, the hut of his mother.

Laying on the Victorian couch, Cocko stared at the ceiling and asked himself quietly, "Why am I a faggot?" Is it because Mother took me for swimming lessons at the Young Women's Christian Association, and made me splash and play with the little girls, wearing a bathing cap just like a girl?

His mother lay upon the skin bed in the dark light of the hut. Outside the tribal drums were sounding louder and the stamping of the men's feet could be heard, as the dance began. His mother lay naked on the skins, awaiting him. He swallowed with difficulty and took a step toward her. The deep beauty scar upon her forehead seemed to be glowing red as if fresh with blood. But it was an old scar, made long ago with a sacred knife, which had carved the coiled body of a snake into the flesh of her forehead.

The High Priestess smiled and removed the jeweled

diadem of the snake and laid it on the table in the center of the gathered Athenian women. She shook her long black hair out. With eyes glistening bright as the ruby orbs of the snake, she said, "Let us begin, ladies. Who shall tell the first tale for our Goddess?"

The ladies looked at one another, and one of them, the wife of a famous orator, spoke up. I shall begin she said. Her body was long and slender within a diaphanous gown. Curling herself crosslegged on a red cushion, she began.

I will tell you of Pisistratus, who married the daughter of Megacles. She was a lovely girl, with creamy breasts and bountiful behind. However, Pisistratus was a father of several sons from a previous marriage and had no wish to produce more offspring. Defying the way of Demeter, our Goddess of Fertility, he made a most unusual request of his beautiful young wife on the wedding night.

I'd like to stick my prick up your ass, thought Cocko. That's how it all began, when I was just a little kid, a gently blossoming fairy playing a childhood game with a friend. May I shove it up your yes you may. Was that the true beginning or did it happen earlier along the way, when Mother refused to cut my lovely Shirley Temple curls? They hung all the way to my shoulders and in those days, baby, it was not fashionable. And they used to sing:

Bobby Shafto's fat and fair
Combing down his silky hair

I was a fat little Shirley Temple faggot, and I certainly got the shafto, right up my bunghole.

"Darling wife," said King Pisistratus, "please kneel upon the bed, lifting your hind-most part toward me." Well, ladies of Athens, you can imagine how confused the daughter of Megacles was, but she wanted to please her husband and so she complied, assuming the strange posture. Apparently her husband preferred to copulate as the bull does, mounting from behind.

"Lower, my King," she said, feeling his member searching in the darkness between her bountiful cheeks.

"No, right here, my dear," said the King, and with a powerful thrust, he shoved his organ into that tiny hole meant for egress, not entry, except in the most jaded relationships, which this, his bride realized, was developing into.

I enjoy it up the ass, reflected Cocko, toying absentmindedly with the ruffled collar of his shirt. I learned the refinement of the position in college. A graduate-engineering student showed me how to get perfect structural balance, laying on my back and pulling my knees up to my chin. A little vaseline on the end of his bean, and up it went, gentlemen, clean and deep—oh, my god, I can feel it still. I had a letter from him recently. He's building bridges for the army and recently fucked a four-star General.

The young warrior knelt beside his mother. The men had instructed him in what he must do with her. He was afraid, was more frightened of this than of sleeping alone in the bush. But his mother was aware of her duty and being everready to cooperate with the tribal elders, whose wisdom far exceeded her own, she reached out and placed her hand upon her son's limp little god, which quickened suddenly at her touch.

"Mother," he said, terrified.

"I am not your mother any longer," she said, massaging his god, his sweet little god, which she had washed and protected for so many years and which was now growing handsome in her hand as the drums sounded and the men sang louder:

Now a man
Tiger-man
A boy without a mother
Is a man.

I like my mother, thought Cocko, drumming his fingers on the arm of the couch. She's loads of fun. When I bought the antique shop, she came to town and we strolled around and had a lovely lunch together at Longchamps. We sat outside at a table by the hedges. Well, isn't there something special about Mother? *M* is for all the many things she gave me—like my neurosis. After lunch we went back to the shop and polished up the china dogs and blew the dust off a painting of Queen Victoria. I sold it for a thousand dollars to an interior decorator. It had such a lovely brass inscription.

Once A Queen Always A Queen

Mother isn't a New Yorker, of course, but that's her charm. She's just a small-town mother of a faggot. Well, it's a gay life, collecting old feather boas for the shop. Of course I'm troubled with hemorrhoids, what with all that hammering up my ass.

The brute, thought the daughter of Megacles, how dare he use me this way, putting his monstrous shaft into my tiny hole which is not meant for such things. Oh, it's so painful, and yet—it is not altogether without certain pleasant sensations which makes it all the more degrading. "Please, King Pisistratus, be—more gentle," she begged, looking over her bare shoulder at the King who was grumbling behind her in the dark. Can you imagine, ladies, one of the most desirable girls in Greece being used this way?

Yes, just a little grease, gentlemen, that's all it takes, and the reluctant lover's asshole opens like a pansy. We even picked out the wallpaper of my apartment together, Mother and me, up at Bloomingdale's. A lovely scene, reproduced from an old Grecian urn. I've had so many compliments on it, and one night, when The Green Cornholer was first whacking my carrot, I even shot on it. The stain is still there.

The mother of the young warrior raised his little god to its full height. It stood black, pounding like the drums outside their hut. How quickly he has grown from a kitten into a tiger. She led him with her hand, bringing him closer to her. Her head was spinning with the drums as if she were one of the circling dancers, whirling and tossing in the moonlight. Oh my tiger-man-boy, sweeter than any husband, be my husband-son now. "Here," she said. "This is what you do." She spread her legs, so that it was open to him, and he came directly to it as the warriors sang and fired off their submachine guns into the sky.

Dangerous is she
But he takes her
With his gun
And breaks her hold.

When I was little, thought Cocko, Mother made me come into the bathroom when she was taking a bath and wash her back. And later, after I'd gotten into my pajamas, we played tiddlywinks together on the bed. Does that make her a bad person? They were just a mother's little tendernesses. I remember a boy, young and delicate, when I first came to New York City. He was sitting in the first-floor window of his room on Seventy-first Street. I was on my way home from work. He made eyes at me, dark Latin eyes, and I was caught in his eyes and pretty soon I was caught up his creamy Cuban bum. He'd just had an enema, his douche he called it. He had talcum powder on his ass cheeks. I believe it was Old Spice. Oh, his ass was smooth as velvet. My velvet summer.

The daughter of Megacles laid her head forward on the royal pillows and King Pisistratus thrust again and again into her oh-so-tender virginal sphincter. And he handled her breasts and thighs lasciviously, exciting her. How embarassing, ladies, to be stuck this way.

I have wandered in the subways at four o'clock in the morning, thought Cocko, looking for my kind of pederast. Of course, it can lead to rather peculiar sensations—like the morning I woke up in a strange bed with a red ribbon on the end of my prick and paper clips fastened to my nipples. I have wandered the city this way, looking for a man. Is it because I am afraid I will not be able to get a hard-on with a woman, me, the Betty Grable of Poopsville, Pennsylvania?

She brought her son-lover's god into her. Boom boom say the drums. Crack crack say the submachine guns. Oh, my little Chief, how strong you are, my little son. What love is mine as I hold my little lover where I bore him. "Now you move," she said, herself moving, so that it entered her deeply.

Do you think that just because Mother made me manicure her toenails we had an unnatural relationship?

So this is the great mystery of the tribe, this soft warm hole which closes so heatedly, like fire, like warm fat from hot meat. I am a tiger-man!

Well, of course Mother and I slept together; whenever I had a nightmare about being chased by a gorilla I called her and she came in and snuggled down next to me. And she said, you are my little rabbit, my little bunny-wunny.

Tiger-man, tiger-man

The hut was filled with shadows. She felt her son's frenzied god deep inside her, so deep she could not believe it was her son. She felt the thousand snakes of the jungle writhing in her and she was afraid of him.

"Oh, my husband," said the daughter of Megacles, "you are—hurting me!" The depraved King bounced her across the bed, howling like a tiger, a royal tiger—for though he was depraved, he was still a King with a very noble standard. And far within her, she felt gathering a peculiar mounting enjoyment, as her body moved like a wild tigress against her will.

One morning I woke up in a gentleman's apartment on Park Avenue and saw my host in the hallway, bending the mailman over the banister.

"Ah," sighed the King, and she felt spurting into her his royal dignitaries, crown, seal, and sovereign signature, but it was in her butt, ladies, where no life could sprout. Nonetheless, ladies of Athens, something in woman's nature is always tickled by such close embrace and suddenly the outraged daughter of Megacles was overcome by a rush of great longing, and she pressed and ground herself on the King's organ, dancing hotly on the end of his scepter.

The jungle was filled with screams and song and gunfire. The warrior boy, the tiger-man, convulsed on top of his mother, biting her shoulder and shooting the stream of his soul. The tigers danced upon the sand. His mother received with a sob this twitching moment of his sudden manhood, and felt him running inside her. The hot juices of her son brought her howling into the grand and sinister moment—she became the jungle. Hmmmmmmmn, she was the Great Queen of Tigers.

Hmmmmmmn, all the black eyes were afire. She swung through the trees, Queen of Monkeys. She slithered through the grass, Queen of Serpents; rose out of the water, shaking her hippo hips. He will go away now and live in the hut of some other woman. But I have known him first, and now he is torn from me.

The daughter of Megacles found the unnatural act enjoyable, in spite of herself, but vowed it would not happen again. When it did, again and again, night after night, she told her father, King Megacles, about the insult to her delicate little behind and the family name. An army was raised and war declared, and King Pisisratus was forced to flee his own country, all because he insisted on using his young wife in so unseemly a fashion.

I had no idea I would actually like being cacked in the ass. But when I came home after that first night with the engineering student, I sat down on the floor in front of the full-length mirror and looked at my happy little ass into which he'd shot a pint of jisom and I said to myself, baby, you are queer. And I wasn't afraid until the night I was arrested for propositioning a plainsclothesman in a subway men's room. I should have known better when I saw him that way, standing so far back from the urinal, and waving his cock around for me to see.

The ladies of Athens applauded the fine story and the teller of the tale raised her gown above her hips, so that her lovely distinguished cheeks were visible. And bending over she rotated her naked buttocks round and round, so that her little beard hung down between her gorgeous thighs, demonstrating exactly how the poor daughter of Megacles had been humped. It was a peculiar and rare display, coming from such a highly stationed lady as the wife of a great orator, but this was the time of the *aischrologia,* the tales of mirth and ecstasy to delight the Goddess Demeter and insure that the nation would be strong with new-born sons. And when the comments and laughter had subsided, another beauty lifted her voice and the next tale was begun.

3

King Candaules sat in his throne room, dreaming idly, for his reign was peaceful and he had much time for reflection. His wife chanced to pass by the door and he was stimulated, as always, by her proud bearing and great natural beauty.

"Is not my wife a rare piece?" he asked his bodyguard, the faithful Gyges, who was at attention on the stairs below the throne.

"Indeed, Your Majesty."

The King was suddenly struck by a charmingly

indecent thought. "You should see her naked."

The bodyguard stiffened with horror.

"Yes, yes," said the King, "it will do you good."

They had just come over from New Jersey into the city and were walking around the Village. "Hey, Chuck," said Vince, "I betcha—I betcha you can't drink a pint of whiskey straight down."

"Why, goddammit, I can drink a pint—*and a half*—straight down."

"All right, I'll buy two pints."

The bodyguard of King Candaules, loyal Gyges, again protested. One never knew, he said, what to expect from a woman once her clothes were off. "Please, sir, I beg of you—your wife is a great beauty. I can see that clearly."

"You shall see it more clearly, my man."

They went into a liquor store in the Village and came out carrying two pints of gin. Laughing and blasting, they walked over to Washington Square Park and settled down on a quiet bench. It was a warm summer night. "Gimme that fuckin' bottle," said Chuck, and unscrewed the top.

"Tonight," said King Candaules, "when she is undressing for bed, you will be hiding behind a nearby door in the shadows, and you will see her remove her cloak and you will observe the splendor of the kingdom."

Chuck put the bottle to his lips and started pouring the white fire down his throat. Goddammit, man, who says I can't drink this stuff right down! Chug-a-lug, chug-a-lug. Flames shot along his chest and to his stomach. Here she comes. The lamplit park grew suddenly dim, then flashed bright white. Wow, some kicker, a bet's a bet and already she's more'n half gone. We come to town to get drunk, didn't we, all the way fum Jersey?

That night, the King showed his bodyguard where to hide, which he did, just before the Queen returned from her bath. She entered, then, wearing a dark robe. She was a Lydian, whose women are known for their great modesty, which is such that they rarely show themselves even to their husbands. Perhaps this was why King Candaules was desirous of having four eyes to arouse his passion.

He set the first pint of gin down, empty. "Gimme . . . gim. . . ." Gim bottle . . . got it . . . drink 'er down . . . fire I'm on fire . . . got dark fast . . . never drunk so fast . . . here's she go, number two, down the . . . down . . . down . . . drinky . . . come over do some drinky . . . look out, here she comes. . . .

Even now, as she bent by the chair, removing her slippers, Gyges, the faithful guardsman, was looking her lovely smooth legs up and down. And as her cloak fell away and her sweet firm breasts appeared, and her belly and her golden mound of hair, the guardsman saw it all. She was indeed an eyeful and an arseful, too, as she turned and walked toward the King's bed.

I kin drink 'er rye down . . . pint an a half I kin . . . drink straight . . . winna bet. . . . "There. . . ." Catch my breath. "A pint an a. . . ." Pint an a . . . gettin' black. Catch my breath. Damn stupid thing to do. But we come over here to drink, didn't we . . . a bet's a bet Christ-amighty!

As the Queen slipped into her dark bed, the

guardsman slipped away from his hiding place. But rare it is that a woman does not know when she is being looked upon, and some subtle instinct caused her to look, just at the moment when the guardsman's distinctive cape fluttered in the doorway and she knew that he had seen her. But she remained silent.

"Chuck, you okay? Hey, kin you hear me, kid? Whatsa matter, Chuck, you won the bet! Yeah, here's your twenty bucks, kid, good ole Chuck."

"You were hiding in the doorway last night," said the Queen the next morning in private audience with her husband's bodyguard, who was unable to hide his shame, mixed as it was with the smallest part of passion which cannot hide itself. "I give you your choice, dear man. Kill King Candaules, and marry me, or die now yourself."

CHRISTAMIGHTY!

King Candaules fell dead in his bed, astonished at the unfavorable turn his little joke had taken. His bodyguard took the crown, reigning beside the woman he had spied upon. Now he no longer had to spy.

The distinguished ladies of Athens clapped their pretty hands, for the story of King Candaules was a favorite amongst them and it had been told well by the lovely weaver of the tale, with suitable pauses, and just for the fun of it she had gradually removed her robe to demonstrate exactly how the Queen had shown herself. So now two of the ladies were naked and it was most delightful to see their breasts and bellies. Women are so rare, even in their smallest gestures, said the Goddess Demeter in a silent whisper to all of them.

The ambulance shrieked wildly up the street and leapt the curbstone at Washington Square Park, but the winner of the pint-and-a-half bet was beyond rescue.

"What happened?" the policeman asked the friend of the deceased.

"We was drinkin' . . . we come over from Jersey for a few drinks. . . ."

4

Another lovely Athenian continued the round of tales, kneeling upon a red cushion, her soft voice that of a thoroughbred Greek.

"I'll tell you what I want, kid," said Mr. Pant, short for Panthella, as he was known officially through his checkbook, out of which came weekly payments to young writers grinding out hot novels for the Pant Publishing Company. "What I want to see—and I want to see it on every page—are the words cock, suck, fuck, and cunt. On every page."

Cock suck fuck cunt. The young writer nodded his head, eager, ready to write anything for money.

I do not know, Women of Athens, whether it was by accident or not that my slave girl, Cyno, met such a curious form of copulation as occurred last year. As you may remember, she was accustomed to walking to the well every day, past a herd of goats.

"On every page and make it juicy. If a guy goes down on a broad, you write about how his tongue. . . ." Mr. Pant put out his own tongue and wriggled it. His bald head was lit from behind by a bright window with small octagonal panes of frosted glass held together by a network of steel. The face he made, long red tongue hanging out, lit by the strangely ornate window, seemed like that of a goat-headed figure of the ancient world.

". . . how his tongue goes right up into her pussy. Cunt hairs, clitty-nibble, anything you can think of. If you don't keep it juicy on every page, I'll have to run some cooze pictures in the book to make it sell and I prefer pure litachoor."

The older goat of the herd, the ram who was the strong and unchallenged leader, had often watched Cyno walking by. Whenever the slave girl passed with a jug of water balanced on her head, the old goat would stare at her with red blazing eyes. Often he would work his hooves in the dirt, spraying clods of earth behind him. And when she passed, he would separate from the other goats and look wistfully after her as her rhythmic step carried her along.

"You write me a book with fuck, suck, cock, and cunt on every page, I'll give you two-hundred-fifty bucks."

"Make it three-fifty."

"If I don't have to use cooze pictures to sell it, three-fifty. Sometimes they come down hard on cooze pictures in your small towns."

One day Cyno offered the attentive goat a morsel of food which was left over from her lunch. Whether she'd been saving it for him or not, I do not know, but he took it from her fingers and swallowed it quickly and when she walked on he followed her. Only the voice of the goatherd and his severe stick made the goat elder desist in following those lovely rolling hips of the slave girl.

"You can use canes, sticks, whips, chains, everything but animals. They came down hard on a dog in Cincinnati last week. *Puppy Love,* it was called, by one of my best writers. I took a chance. The Cincinnati Smut Mothers got wind of it and hit me with a court injunction. I wind up with a warehouse full of *Puppy Love,* it costs me money."

One day, the goat began to sing as Cyno approached, rough guttural music breaking from his lips when he saw her. He stopped directly in front of her on the path. She smiled at this strange song, but she dared not laugh for his eyes were fierce and he was clearly not joking. And when she attempted to pass him, he blocked her path with lowered horns.

"How soon you think you can have a book for me, kid?"

"A week," said the young writer as he left the Pant

Publishing house, his briefcase loaded with sample books which had fuck suck cock cunt on every page.

She drew back frightened as the goat nudged her gently with his head. She moved to the left; he moved with her. To the right and he was there. She backed up and he was upon her, tossing her gown up with demoniacal agility, so that her legs and belly were bare. She cried, but the goatherd was not to be seen and indeed it was just such a chance the goat elder had been waiting for. He brought his hooves upon her arms, and then, with his horns, rolled her over. The poor girl was afraid to move or crawl. Or perhaps it was not altogether a matter of fear, who knows?

He wrote all week with a boner and felt strange and furious presences in his shabby room.

Overpowered by the goat, she could only hold fast to the sand as he mounted her, driving the long thin red shining member of his species into her astonished cunt.

"Jesus Christ, kid, I told you—no animals!"

"It just came naturally."

"Maybe," said Mr. Pant, "we can pass it off as a ribald classic. I got nothin' against goats personally."

5

The working-class girls of Lydia, said the next speaker, have a custom quite unlike anything in our homeland. Without exception, they prostitute themselves in order to build up a handsome dowry for their marriage. Their fathers are responsible for this practice, for they wish their daughters to marry well. My story is of one such daughter, Lyca, and her father Mylus.

Lyca was darkly beautiful and commanded a fine price for her favor. The handsomest of men could not turn her head, unless it was with a gift of a ruby-studded fan or comb. Only then would she present to him her own spread fan of soft design.

She looked out her window to Prince Street below. Night was coming on the lower edge of Greenwich Village. She put on a white shirt and slacks, combing her short hair into a ducktail in back. Upon her wrist was a heavy identification bracelet, bearing the name Spike. She wore no makeup, her eyebrows were unplucked, and her body was not graceful as she strode back and forth before her mirror assuming masculine postures. In her eyes was a cold and fiercely burning look, which she remembered having always, even as a little girl. Now, in her late twenties, it had become her strongest point of identity, for in those eyes she saw the man she felt herself to be. The fierce burning was the bitterness of this man who had been cast by fate into the body of a woman, prickless and titful.

Tucking her shirt further into her pants, she flattened her bosom, but the shirt worked itself loose by the time she stood on the street below and her clumsy breasts were all too apparent once again. She had a little money from the factory on Canal Street, where she worked assembling small electric switches every day with several Puerto Rican women. She had enough money for a Friday night in the bar.

Lyca was wealthy from selling her pleasures and for the right price she would do anything within the range of human desire. It was this, along with a characteristic perversity, that led her father, Mylus, to the very inferno of taboo, directly into the jaws of incest. He arranged through another party that he should visit his own daughter, himself masked and she blindfolded, so that she might never know that he had slept with her.

Lyca accepted the curious request that she receive a masked man and be herself covered in darkness as they screwed. It made no odds to her how the deed was done so long as it was well paid for, and she already had the heavy sack of gold in her hands, given to her by messenger. My customer must be some man of public office, she reasoned, who does not wish himself known to me. And so she prepared a blindfold of deep black material like the face of night.

Up East Broadway she walked, toward Washington Square Park. The Park would be filled with strange seekers like herself. The sound of drums and singing came through the trees. Her world was small, the Village her territory, and she did not enjoy leaving it. The Park was the center of that world, where numerous half-men, half-women hung out. She'd find a girl; there was always a girl. But even the thought of finding and loving in the night did not extinguish the cold burning in her eyes, caused perhaps by the narrowness of her world—the Village, a few square blocks of bars and cafés, inside of which she stalked like a caged and nervous animal.

Lyca put her mask on and lay upon her bed. The serving boy brought her guest into the room. The room was covered with heavy rugs, so that her guest's footsteps were absorbed into dark silence and all was dark behind her blindfold. But she could feel him coming, and sensed a peculiar intensity in his approach. She knew men's souls, for she'd been consort to many, and she knew that this man was powerfully moved and powerfully moving.

Mylus walked like a blind man, led by the serving boy's hand, his heart filled with warring emotions. His daughter awaited him, his very flesh—hellish step! And yet, ever since she was a child how fascinated he'd been by her beauty, and the love he bore her was a painful ache of longing near to madness. He had resisted it nobly until she had become a courtesan. Then, hearing from other men the great skill his daughter had in love-making, he could deny himself the pleasure no longer. But it must be masked, for this love is cursed and blind. And so he came to the edge of her bed.

She stood at the circular fountain in the Park, listening to the drumming music. Streams of people went by in all directions and she searched the stream for the face that would smile or the eyes that would answer. She'd come from Ohio, she'd ridden the night train to Grand Central Station, she'd learned to wear a rubber dildo, and she'd realized that her life would be a bittersweet fuck. That was all right; she could take cheap bars and the secret painful longing. She could sit all night in a coffeehouse, she was on her own, she could watch the night walk by, and nobody could push her around. But she felt her anger welling up anyway, unnamable and wild, aimed at someone unknown.

"You do not speak to me?" asked Lyca as her suitor-customer sat upon the bed. Who can it be who will not speak? Is it a well-known orator whose voice would reveal him? He did not speak, except with his fingertips, which gently touched her leg. How gentle he is, how rare his caress. She was used to more coarse advances and this was so timid. Is he young? She reached out, felt his hand. No, it was not the hand of a youth. He is a man, then, with a secret. Well, we all have our little secrets, she thought, and she opened her gown so that he could feel the treasure.

The Park was lit by bright streetlamps, and passing through the light were couples and gangs, lonesome travelers, and freaks. She was a freak, too, a special kind of freaky being in a man's shirt and trousers, in plain shoes, with chewed-down fingernails and hunched-over shoulders. She stood, hands in her pockets, a cigarette dangling from her lips. She took a deep breath, and straightened up, resting her foot on the rim of the fountain in that casual masculine air she felt was her secret self, and which she worked so hard to make real. I'm a New York City dike, that's how it goes, baby. The little ache of sadness came and she smiled it away, off and away at no one on the summer night. That little ache seemed made of party dresses and doll's underclothes, things from long ago that threatened her, rising up in her heart, where she could only suffer them without a word. This suffering, the bitter and distant smile that marked it, was for her a test of her masculinity. She had the strength to bear that ache, to smile past it, roughly, toughly, like a hero, a French-film gangster—anything—so long as she did not succumb to the sadness and weep like a woman. The gentle summer wind blew her close-cropped hair in fine wisps on her forehead, and she walked along the edge of the fountain to where a crowd had gathered, listening to a black singer who played a guitar that had only one string on it. A freak, a wanderer, that's what we all are.

Mylus lingered on the body of his daughter with his fingers, touching it not as men touch for the first time on a foreign shore, with self-abandon, but savoring all the little hills and valleys like a sailor returning to a familiar land, a land well known and long lost.

Fascinated by this exquisite attention, and not a little stirred, the pulse of Lyca quickened as he touched her there and there, and, finally, there.

"You are gentle," she said, receiving him into her, into the secret room of her profession which she had lathered with cream to make certain all fit well without tension or dryness. She looked into her black blindfold and wondered at her lover, and her wonder increased as he entered fully, for his member was radiant, as if the fire of Apollo himself had burned her.

Mylus sank into the depth of his despair of desire, the vagina of his daughter; the little dream he'd nourished sprang into awesome fulfillment. And he remembered that many men had enjoyed her and his pleasure increased. She is love's fair game for he who has the price; thus did he crush the incestuous taboo. In ritual awakening, then, he pushed his member again and again into his beloved daughter and she responded with little cries, most alarming to the ears of her serving boy, who was not accustomed to such outbreaks of emotion from his mistress. But he waited, as always, outside her door, knowing that she could handle any man.

But Lyca was in the grip of an emotion stronger than any she'd known in her career. Could it be that she, the golden prostitute, had met her destiny in this blind masquerade? Her dowry was full, fuller than any other working girl of the town or any other near town. She was free to choose her husband, which was custom with those women who have earned their own fortune.

"I have much to give," she whispered, as he made his love to her. His answer was a convulsive shudder of emotion which quickened her conviction that he was the one, that a fateful crossing had taken place in the dark. She knew deeply, instinctively, that this was the man, the only man. And love, which hides itself in the whore, leapt forth in her heart, swelling her breast. "I am yours," she said, embracing him, raising her knees up and surrounding him with her legs. "And you are mine. I know this. It comes to me from the gods, my lover, do not doubt it."

The crowd grew larger around the singer and she smiled as she listened to his high-pitched street voice, singing a dark Harlem song. And then the close press of bodies in the crowd grew more than casual. She felt suddenly, upon her rear, at the seat of her trousers, a hand, taking hold of her, and she turned like a fighting cock, spurs glistening, fists raised, seeing his face, a punk, a big stupid crew-cut smiling son of a bitch and her deep burning flame of hate rose up in her. With the rage of years, she punched him so hard in the face they both fell to the ground, he flat on his back and she on top of him. "Keep your hands off the women!" she cried, and when he struggled to rise she drilled him again, straight in the nose, and had to be dragged off him and was held in the crowd as he quickly got up and ran off, holding his nose and losing himself in the shadows. She was breathing wildly, her heart pounding madly, but she was filled with a screaming joy as if her woman's body had finally fallen away and her manhood been declared, miraculously. Strong arms held her as she struggled to free herself, and she felt like a prize fighter. When they released her, there was laughter and she looked around quickly, but no one, man or woman, returned her gaze. And she walked on along one of the many sidewalks of the Park, past the benches filled with people, and the chess tables where the click-click of the pieces could be heard in the silent air of the games.

How surprised was Lyca, ladies of Athens, when her mysterious lover, to whom she had just declared her secret heart, leapt from her with a cry of pain such as she had never heard from man, woman, or beast. The masked man fled from her chamber, into the night, leaving her with a love broken in its first moment.

6

Ladies of Athens, said the next speaker, we must remember our sweet strength and rejoice in it. As Father Plutarch has said, flute girls have trampled on the diadems of kings. And such is the tale I will spin for you now.

Every night after leaving work, he walked along Forty-second Street to his favorite bookstore. In the back of the store were a series of rooms devoted to different aspects of voyeurism and he went habitually to his favorite, a small closetlike room with a window in it. This window was darkened and covered by a drape. Alongside it was a coin slot, and by inserting a quarter into the slot he triggered the drapes, which then rolled open, revealing beyond, an adjoining room. In this room was a rotating platform upon which a live model lay, naked.

Her name was Semiramis, and she was the concubine of a slave boy belonging to King Nimus. The slave treated her well, for she was exceedingly lovely with dark Syrian breasts, ruby-tipped in soft nipples. She knew how to dress herself with beads and lengths of fine gauze, so that every one of her charms seemed to show itself, here and there, behind a bead, which might suddenly swing asunder, revealing the proud puppy nose of her breast. With such bodily splendor she kept the poor slave in a constant state of weariness, draining from him every ounce of his manhood. Well, she was a slave girl, and what else was she to do with the long hot day but tempt him, and spank him with her thighs, and make him so wan he seemed a dying moon.

At the sight of her through the window, he opened his belt buckle and lowered his trousers and shorts. But the curtains closed again moments later and he had to insert another quarter to open them once more. Staring hungrily at the naked girl, who assumed various indecent postures, he began to pound his lonely boner, making panting sounds as he did so. And then as the quarter was expired and the curtain closed again, he desisted with a moan, not wanting to shoot quickly and so soon bring about the end of his after-work cocktail hour. He inserted another quarter and the curtain opened again.

The great King Nimus, descended from magnificent blood, fierce as a lion, ravenous as a crow, subtle as a lizard frozen in contemplation of an insect, stared at the slave girl Semiramis who casually paraded herself past his open throne room. He had her summoned to him immediately, had the doors closed behind them, had her strip, and had her.

But Semiramis was no ordinary wench. She was born with that rare freedom of body, rare even in woman, resulting in orgiastic thrashing and calling, weeping and squirming, such that her lover thinks he has fallen into bed with ten women at once. King Nimus was astounded and for a moment childishly feared for his life, so powerful were the undulations beneath him, and the love bites and the fingerings and squeezings and every other trick of a slave-girl Semiramis with a plan.

The little man in the dark watching-room beat his meat with gentle strokes, trying to hold it back, wanting to raise his joy just to the brim and hold it there while he raised some more right behind it. He was a jack-off expert, knew exactly how to wind the maximum semen out of his member. The curtains closed again and he relaxed the grip on his throbbing dobber. With all his perceptive powers fixed on the girl who rotated beyond him on the platform, he was scarcely aware of the little dark room he himself sat in, and consequently was not cognizant of the two eyes which peered at him through a special slit in the wall, carefully arranged by the management. Here, watching the man who watched the rotating girl, was another man, who paid fifty cents. The extra twenty-five cents thus included a view of the distant girl beyond the draped window, and the man jacking off in her honor in the adjacent room.

"You are wonderful," said the King to Semiramis, when their first round of desire had peeked and passed.

"I am only a slave's toy," she said, toying with the King.

"You have become the most important woman in my country," said the King. "There is no one who is your equal."

"No, no," she said "I am just a bright little gem of no real significance. You, my King, are the King of jewels." And so saying, she fondled those precious jewels which do not sparkle, except within, where they are liquid and fiery crystal.

The King, sighing, said, "Whatever you wish is yours, little gem."

"Then let me wish for the ridiculous," said Semiramis. "Let me sit upon your throne and wear the diadem and direct the state for a day."

The King consented. They played a bit more and he gave more of the royal seed into her dark earth. All afternoon they delighted, and Semiramis sucked away into herself all the life power of the ruler, until he was lying weak on the deep carpet, giggling happily, near stupification from the drain she had placed on his manhood. Then she, bursting with Kingly semen, said sweetly, "May I now assume the throne?"

"Yes, yes," he said, laughing, his breath short and strained.

And she rose up to the throne, placed the diadem on

her head, and assumed the stature of royalty. The King laughed again to see her sitting there, so bold and beautiful. Women, he reflected, are like children. How they love to play.

Panting crazily, the jack-off artist whipped a tissue out of a box, thoughtfully provided by the management to avoid excess blobs of jisom on the floor, which might make someone slip and fall. The artist placed the tissue to his boner, took a last fervent, gasping look at the rotating girl and came, stretching out on his chair. In front of his eyes he saw a hundred women and they were all his and it was so sweet and sad, so warm and awful, so over and done with. Lost in fantastic passion, he did not hear the turning of the sixteen-millimeter camera, which was focused on him through a careful flower arrangement placed by the management. He did not know he was a star! Soon he would be sold in many copies over and under the counter to frustrated housewives, to film societies, to varying and sensitive collectors and cinema buffs all over the globe. His name in lights! Advertised in thrilling adventure men's magazines, the kind men like and women too! The leading lady and himself, starring in:

MASTURBATION TECHNIQUES
FOR YOU

A scientific study by a well-known professional nurse inclusive of the male and female anatomy for beginners

$4.95

(*mailed in plain brown wrapper, of course*)

He wiped his pulsing prick, placed it back in his pants, and skulked out of the store into the street. He'd have to get straight over to Grand Central Station or he'd miss his train. It was already dark and his wife would have supper on the table.

Semiramis held the royal scepter in her hand and King Nimus guffawed. How lovely she is on my throne with her lovely legs, and clear eyes. She has all my juices, they make her eyes shine like that, like a queen. Listen to her, calling for the Royal Guard. She sounds just like a sovereign.

The guardsmen of King Nimus appeared, six strong, in armor and weapons, marching carefully past the reclining King and taking their position at the foot of the throne. The concubine-queen smiled with cold authority. "Arrest that man who lies there so irreverently and place him in chains."

Without batting an eyelash, the guardsmen seized the King, who was so lately their master. "Let me go, you idiots!" he cried. "This is just a game! Let me go, or I'll have you destroyed on the instant. Let me. . . ."

But the diadem and scepter are the Syrian symbols of royalty, and Semiramis held them as naturally as if she'd always done so. And if the King was so naïve as to bestow them upon such a woman, then perhaps he was not the wisest of rulers. But Semiramis was indeed wise and with much sagacity did she rule over Asia for many years.

7

The next speaker was a dark-eyed beauty who stretched her legs casually, allowing her gown to fall open to her crotch, which was covered in dark luxurious curls, neatly trimmed. Women of Athens, she said, please remember Mais, the grand prostitute of our city, who had lovers of every kind. In the forest of fornication she was a fertile tree, allowing herself to bear one son every five years from the man who pleased her most, be he soldier, lawmaker, or stripling. Her chamber was a red-hung room with deep silks and tapestries of many lands surrounding her as she lay beneath her customers, performing her sacred duty.

Forty-ninth Street was still good for a last trick, and she walked along it in a mini-skirt which barely covered her ass. Her stomach was gaseous from drinking too much phony champagne. Just one more trick before bed, and she saw him now, looking guilty and horny, standing in front of the Cuckātoo Club, a B-girl bar he didn't have the guts to go into or the brains to stay away from.

It happened that a soldier of our Athenian army was searching for Mais. He asked an old man of the whores' quarter where she lived.

"That's where you'll find her, sir," said the old man, pointing to the house of Mais. "And she is very fine, indeed."

"I have heard," said the soldier, "that she has great virtue."

"It may be so, sir, but I believe that a certain vice is her virtue."

The soldier was shown into the chambers of the prostitute, who received him upon her golden couch.

"Hi ya, honey," she said.

"Oh, hello," said the John in front of the bar, turning toward her, his eyes lighting up.

"You look lonesome."

"Think you can help that?"

"I can try."

He extended his arm to her and they walked along the street.

All around the prostitute, Mais, were arranged peacock

feathers, said to be bad luck for lovers. The elderly captain of the army said, "Madame, I have need of a woman's sagacity."

"Come to me on my couch, Captain," said Mais. "I cannot receive you into my confidence until I take you in my arms. Come, old battleman, come to battle with Mais."

The man stopped on the corner of Forty-ninth Street and Broadway. "Right here," he said, pointing to a long black car in which another man was waiting.

"Oh, no, honey, no joy rides for mama."

"You'll take this ride, sister," he said, flashing his badge and opening the door with the same motion.

"You lousy son of a bitch." She tore her arm away from his, but he pushed her into the back seat.

The captain went to her upon the couch then, and felt beneath him the soft and studied loveliness of the courtesan's art. She soothed him and stroked him and as they loved, she said quietly, "What problem is in your heart, Captain?"

"Many vessels are proceeding upriver to attack us. I know of no oracle to whom I can speak. We are greatly outnumbered. How should our defense be made?"

"There is one certain defense against annihilation which the prostitute knows," said Mais.

They drove down Broadway toward the House of Detention. She sat in a heap in the corner of the back seat of the car.

"Whatsa matter, baby," said the vice cop. "Cat got your tongue?"

"Fuck off, buster."

"A tough number. We'll see how tough you are, honey," he said, and gave a coarse laugh, spitting out the window of the unmarked squad car.

The captain felt a sudden rocking of his body as on an ocean which spreads out and out. The soft white breast of the prostitute floated him. Her eyes were dark and ravishing like the peacock's, and her lips were red as rose-hips. Like a man waking from a dream, he looked at the woman beneath him and was dazzled.

The squad car pulled up to the station house; they took her up the stone steps and through the door, leading her to the desk of the night officer. "Hooking on Forty-ninth Street," said the arresting officer.

She was silent now, down in the coldness that was her real heart, where the freaks couldn't touch her. She had that, anyway, whatever in hell it was, a piece of ice, maybe, because it never melted.

"All men are the same, Captain," said Mais, as she rocked her lover. "That is the harlot's truth." And even as the prostitute spoke, the approaching invader felt the tremor of her truth, for the waters of the river began churning as if a giant swarm of fish had begun to dance. It is said by the Delphinian oracles that any being who has mastered one portion of the vast truth of existence has the power to control certain elemental forces. And this is what the accomplished prostitute, lovely Mais, was doing.

"Yes, Captain," she said, "all men are one. My body will testify to that equality."

The townspeople looked on with gaping eyes as did the threatening soldiers. The tide of the river was turning. Mud appeared; the veil of water curled itself, rolling backstream from whence it came as if pushed by a powerful wind.

She was led to a small bare room by the arresting officer. "Lift up your skirt."

"There's no policewoman here, punk. I'm not lifting my skirt for any little freak like you."

"I said, lift it, bitch!"

Moving back from his clenched fist, she dropped into the ice, lifting her dress as if in a bad dream. She was not really there. She was somewhere far off, watching the hungry sick son of a bitch popping his eyes at the sight of her stockings and white thighs. She wasn't there and never would be. Maybe the ice inside me is death. I carry my death inside me, wherever I go.

The captain of the army left the house of the courtesan, carrying with him the memory of her moon-white thigh. If I must die this night defending against the invader, it will be a good night for death. He was met by a breathless runner of his army.

"The river, Captain. Most amazing, sir."

"Yes, what is it?"

"Turned backwards, sir, and held itself that way as if some mighty force had stopped its flowing."

The vice-squad cop took hold of her panties with his hand. "Let's see if you're carrying any dope, baby," he said, yanking down her panties hurriedly.

"Let me alone, you fucking creep." Like a scared kid, the cop shoved his finger up her ass.

The captain rushed on through the moonlit night to the river's edge. It was flowing again, as it always had, rushing darkly through the night. But the enemy torches which had approached earlier in the evening were extinguished, and there was no sound of the threatening invader.

"I swear it, Captain," said the boy. "Many of us saw it happen. Their ships were swept under and tossed back to the sea."

She let him wiggle his finger up her ass, his thumb clumsily hurting her. She stood it and had no tears, not even anger. It would do her no good to report him; a whore had no chance in this House. And in the desperate grip of his gorilla finger, she recognized the same old lover, the one she'd come to know so well on each and every night.

Welcoming the next customer into her red-draped room, Mais, our city's most distinguished prostitute, was brand-new for him as if no past had soiled her body. She seemed a virgin, though but an hour ago she had conceived a child by the captain of the army. She remembered his visit with secret pleasure, however, and later that year she gave his child to the temple of the Delphi oracle. The child was there initiated into the sacred ways as one who has been conceived without shame.

8

The High Priestess of the temple lifted her voice, then, to begin the next tale of the night. It is the custom in Babylonia, she said, that sometime in her life every woman must go to the temple of Aphrodite and give herself to a stranger. The temple is always filled and the women wait in long rows. The man indicates his choice by tossing a coin into the woman's lap and she cannot refuse him. Thereupon they proceed to a nearby field and commence fucking.

She'd had many bosses in the company, and she refused

to be their doormat and told them so. She refused to get them coffee and doughnuts in the morning. "I'm not a maid, Mr. So-and-so," she would say, and not long after she would be transferred to some other executive. Down the line she went, until she became secretary to a strange and tortured man, a genius copywriter, whose stomach problems eliminated her problem of having to bring him pastry and coffee in the morning. His only food the entire day consisted of a few pieces of fruit, eaten at lunch. Strange as was his diet, he was the most powerful copywriter in the business, the one who had penned the most famous direct-mail letter of all time, which began:

Dear Sir:
Let me release a roaring river of riches into your life.

His own problem was the release of a roaring torrent of pain through his bowels—a stomach ailment which visited him daily and which he barely held in check by his fruit diet. His quiet anguish touched a sympathetic nerve in his secretary, and she became devoted to him.

She went to the temple of Aphrodite with eager footsteps. She had no husband, for she was not pretty. Her only affair had been a drunken moment with a slave, many years before when she was an even homelier adolescent. So now, with desire having mounted year after year in her body, and with no sign of a lover in view, she went to the temple to be chosen by a stranger. Gayly she set out in her best tunic with perfumes and her one piece of jewelry, a gold bracelet in the shape of a serpent which spanned her wrist. As she approached the temple, and saw the bright colors of the women's gowns, and so many of them, her step faltered. As she drew directly near and saw the beauties ahead of her, waiting in line to be chosen, her heart sank and her embarrassment increased. With all these beauties available, the most beautiful women of Babylon, who would pick her, a homely horse-faced thing?

"Will there be anything else today, Mr. Comola?" The efficient Miss Radcliff stood beside the desk of the tortured genius copywriter. They'd worked together a year now, in which time he'd written hundreds of selling letters of extraordinary persuasiveness, near-magical, containing fantastic hypnotic suggestions which had increased his company's profits considerably. Yet with women he had no powers, no suave line, no professional approach. He'd almost resigned himself to celibacy until Miss Radcliff came along and she brought his passion alive again. Often, while composing roaring rivers of sales pitches, his eyes were fixed on her crossed legs, a desk away from him.

He would follow the smooth ascent of her leg, from ankle to knee, and occasionally, when she made a sudden move, swinging out of her posture chair, he saw DIRECTLY UP THE GOLDEN RIVER OF HER THIGHS! Let me repeat that for you, sir, so that you will recognize the utter seriousness of this offer—HER THIGHS AND SOMETIMES EVEN A GLIMPSE OF HER PINK PANTIES!

His genius thought to win her as it had won millions

of junk-mail readers across the land to buy junk books written by crackpots and con artists, racetrack touts and religious lunatics, whom his company had sought out and contracted. Whenever a screwball of any sort appeared with an ad in a religious newspaper (his company subscribed to them all) or in *Far Out Space* magazine, his copy chief wrote that screwball a letter and said, *Dear Sir, would you like to write a book for us on your marvelous system of telling fortunes from a used tissue?*

When the manuscript was submitted, it would be incomprehensible. It was then turned over to the college-trained editorial staff who put it into workable English. The genius copywriter Comola would then spin a fantasy letter of promise about this book to men and women everywhere in America.

With such a background of selling a worthless product in a difficult way, he had prepared himself for the supreme moment which had now come. Trembling all over, he typed out a note and handed it to his secretary, the attentive Miss Radcliff. It read:

Dinner tonight. I'll pick you up at eight.

She took her seat by the golden statue of Aphrodite and watched the priests and priestesses serving food to the waiting women, for it was necessary that guests of the Goddess eat and drink. The good food and wine were purchased through offerings of gold made to the temple by the Babylonian nobility. And so she ate a delicious meal and every time a man passed her, she tried to present him her best feature, a lovely ankle. But he always passed and tossed his gold coin into the lap of a beauty. She sat and waited—a day, a month, a year.

She'd had dates with other company men, but they were all so pompous and filled with themselves. Mr. Comola, Jim, was shy and much the best man among them. So she went home, almost on a cloud, though a working girl always has to keep her feet at least skimming over the ground. She prepared for him slowly and carefully, bathing in warm bubbles, and put on an especially alluring red dress never worn to the office. Making herself up in the mirror, she hummed a little song and already, far back in her mind, was a faint picture of life on a permanent basis with Jim Comola. Her eyes brightened, edged in tiny lines of artful black, and smoothly worked shadows of blue.

Not for an entire year did she receive a glance from a stranger. She could have left the temple, of course, and escaped into more discreet loneliness, but she chose to stay at the temple of Aphrodite, for it had occurred to her that she could find no better treatment anywhere and the statue of the Goddess was lovely to look at. She dreamed on it, day after day, for the entire second year of her stay. Becoming friendly with the priestess of the temple, she occasionally was allowed to participate in incantations to the Goddess, reciting secret prayers of devotion. It relaxed her, dissolved her tension and made her less mindful of her homeliness.

He'd had a little fruit for lunch, just a few oranges, an

apple, and some grapes, but then with a daring burst of recklessness he bought a candy bar of a soft gooey substance, which he ate in well-chewed bites. The thought of Miss Radcliff inspired this rash act and new courage was his. The roaring river of love was flowing in his heart. But so too was the wretched river of shit in his bowels, and while on the subway toward her apartment he was suddenly struck by a terrible pain in the guts, as if someone had clenched his bowels in a tight fist, a demonic little fist which squeezed tighter and tighter. He'd been through it before countless times. In the middle of the night, he'd often leapt out of bed and raced to the bathroom, where he died until dawn with cramps that made him scream, *please, no*. The river in his body was polluted by some little demon of fierce campaigns, who shot balls of crap out of his ass until it bled. And now, on the way to HER house, on the IRT subway, he hurt down low, oh, no, please, no.

He went quickly through the open subway doors and through the turnstyle, holding his sphincter muscle with a difficult effort, for cannonades were going off in his intestines, building up super gasses, enough to destroy the Third Reich and England if released. Jesus, why me? Why do I have to bear this? He hurried up the subway steps to the street. I must get to a toilet immediately. A glowing river of shit. Success can be yours if you can find a place to release it. Women will throw themselves at your feet. Not a toilet in sight. Not a restaurant in this neighborhood, no gas station; drugstores do not have crappers. For just $3.95 I will send you, on a money-back guarantee, a book that will make you a superman, a titan of power, a giant among men, must get to a toilet, could have used the subway one for a dime but it stinks so badly and I might be accosted there. Foolish pride. Swallow it. Go straight to Miss Radcliff's house. She is your secretary, she understands. Don't ask questions, Miss Radcliff, I must get to your bathroom. She's often seen me half-trotting down the hallway of the office, crimping my ass cheeks together as I ran. A grand girl, a perfect woman, the one and only glowing river. $3.95. Terrible pain in the ass.

And as he walked, even through his misery, he felt that with the relieving of his problem in her bathroom, he would break down one of his silly inhibitions, like not being able to piss if anyone was nearby. Often he'd stood at a public urinal, frozen, unable to activate his urine. He'd look at the ceiling and whistle nonchalantly as if he were pissing gallons like a real piss-and-vinegar American, but the pee in his dong would be blocked up like the entrance to the Pharaoh's tomb. Hidden passageways of the mind, secrets revealed, just $3.95, send today.

I'll go straight to her place. Lovely night for an exploding bowel. Straight up this street, walking fast, not too fast, mustn't draw attention to myself and be stopped by a policeman for questioning. Any delays and I'm in trouble, friend, bad trouble.

Homely as she was, her adoration of the beautiful Goddess made her feel beautiful inside and presently this feeling of beauty began to manifest itself upon the surface. Our waiting lady felt the difference as if another person was being born in her every pore. This is the gentle and subtle insinuation of the divine being, ladies of Athens. The girl's appearance began to change! Her meager hips took on weight, her bust flowered, her cheeks bloomed, even her hair lost its frizzy contradictoriness as if some delicate wave from within had changed the field of her energies, redirecting their movement in beautiful patterns. She was becoming a siren.

With feverish urgency he rang the bell in the lobby of her apartment house. A roaring river of turds is waiting in your lobby, please, sound the entrance buzzer and let me in and I'll make you a King at the Racetrack!

BZZZZZZZZZZZ. He pushed at the door, its lock yielding to the electric impulse from her fingertip, three flights above. The elevator? No, too risky. Might get stuck between floors. Disaster if that happened.

The apartment house was strange to him, but he climbed the stairs with familiarity born of desperation. A glowing river of carpeted stairs to the BATHROOM OF YOUR DREAMS! Intestines backing up, building tremendous pressure in lower abdomen, creating dangerous waves of near-farts. Must control asshole. He walked bravely up the steps, resolutely shoving his thumb up hard into the seat of his pants, pressing it like a cork into his burning, churning sphincter.

I am beautiful, she thought with amazement, looking at herself in the mirror of the temple priestess. How has this happened, she asked herself. She was undeniably beautiful, after years of homely unhappiness. Now she might get herself a stranger, anyone she chose. But she remained with the temple and became its Priestess, showing young girls how to make themselves into their true image, which is inevitably beautiful but masked by pain and doubt.

The hallway of the third floor presented a devilish trap of intersecting doorways. Finger still jammed up his glowing asshole, he took a wrong turn, going in the opposite direction from apartment sixteen, her apartment, going all the way to the other end of the hall before noticing his mistake.

Help. Mommy, Daddy, why? Simply by dropping the enclosed postage-paid order form in a mailbox, you will insure yourself against psychic warfare, cruelly played upon you by THOSE WHO HATE YOU. I'm sure you know someone like that, who dislikes you intensely. Learn the SCIENCE OF PSYCHIC JUDO! Give me, quick, please, one toilet. I'll pay anything, $3.95, you name it, it's yours, simply think with all your might about what you want and my amazing PSYCHIC POWER-PAC will produce it, one toilet, please produce it, where is her apartment. There . . . that way . . . fourteen–fifteen–sixteen.

He rang the bell. He heard her footsteps approaching through his agony. He saw their entire life together, stretching out before them, a glowing river of tenderness, priceless, joyful. Hurry with the door, please. Don't waste time, don't waste a single moment, please, the pain, the atom-bomb fart.

"Hello, Jim," she said, opening the door.

He removed his thumb from his asshole and shit

himself on her doorstep, a thunderous volley of wet farting cucky, uncontrollable, abominable, all over himself, high stink, now let me die.

"I've just shit in my pants," he said as calmly as he could, "may I please use your bathroom?"

9

Our Goddess, ladies of Athens, in whose honor we have gathered here this evening, is both the Queen of Fertility and the Guardian of the Social Order, especially that institution of marriage which she will not suffer to be scorned. First let me make myself comfortable by removing my gown, and now I shall tell you how seven distinguished Persian soldiers tasted Demeter's wrath.

Persia had the upper hand of Macedonia in combat: Persian envoys came to receive an offering of earth and water from the Macedonians, who arranged for a splendid banquet. It was hoped that genial hospitality would soften the oppression which was being visited on the Macedonians by their Persian conquerors. The Persians, however, were disturbed by the absence of any women at the banquet and made their complaint. It is not the custom for Macedonian women to sit with men, but an exception was made and they were brought from their private chambers.

The prize fag of Pothole, Pennsylvania, left his furnished room and traveled the few blocks to his main drag in the black section of town. He was there every night—a middle-aged queen, with beauty-parlored hair waved in silver ringlets, his lips red as neon. He was called Mister Sam.

"How ya doin', Mister Sam," asked the black grocer man, coming to stand outside his shop in the hot summer night.

"Fine, just fine," said Mister Sam, smiling at the black man. Pothole was Mister Sam's town, and he was its blow job. He liked it that way, being the celebrity. There was always someone coming around, some curious youngster wanting to see a real live fag, and if they came to see they could also come in his mouth; that's how Mister Sam looked at the situation. He'd had some wonderful moments with young men, too numerous to count, but sometimes he saw their pictures on the sports page, or later, in the society column with their fiancées, and he would smile. Nice boys, boys he had blown out on back roads, parked in the dark. Life was very good that way; it sent him many gifts. He looked upon himself as a teacher—a gentle old practitioner of the art of blowing. He brought the young men out. *"There,"* he had often said, lifting his head off of some boy's squirming lap, *"now you're a man."*

"Very well," said the Persian captain, "is it to look upon your wives, dear Macedonians, but must they be so separated from us? We sit here, with our full stomachs and our wine glasses full, and they sit across from us like screened-off hens. Surely we can all mix and mingle socially as our countries will in future." He had his eye on one particular beauty with golden hair and sumptuous breasts.

The Macedonian chief considered it a bad business, letting his wife and the wives of his sons and brothers and countrymen mix with the Persians. But such is the subservience that grows in a conquered man's heart that he did that which he despised doing, and allowed his wife to be seated by a dark swarthy Persian, who immediately touched her breast.

A shiny customized car with several young boys in it came slowly by, and Mister Sam looked coquettishly at them. Yes, it was getting time. They'd all been drinking for a few hours and now they were looking for kicks. But they went on by, without stopping. "They'll be back," he said, puckering his lips, kissing the night. "They always circle around."

"They got to come in slow," said the grocer, scratching his back against the doorframe.

"Your toes, madame, are exquisite little ivories such as Persia never possessed, even amongst its greatest beauties." The Captain reached for more wine and touched her on the toes. She was frightened and he enjoyed it, for behind her fear he was certain of that one frailty which we women are known to suffer—we go weak with a man, any man, if he is persistent enough. He may be gross, a misshapen wretch, an impudent slave, a powerful barbarian whose breath smells of foul meals and deeds, but something in our nature is beyond such distinctions. Something answers, no matter how fickle or dangerous or distasteful the call may seem to our conscious selves. And so, because the serpent can excite us easily, Demeter has seen fit to protect us.

"And your neck, madame, is like a swan, so white and smooth," said the captain, touching her there.

Mister Sam's hair sparkled in the light of the storefront, sprayed with a fixative that held his waves in place like those of a Greek statue. But his body was not cast from the Greek mold of beauty; he had small narrow shoulders, a flabby chest, and a potbelly. He never counted on his looks, except for his coiffure and lipstick. That was all the honey the boys needed.

"Here they come again," said the grocer.

"Boys will be boys," said Mister Sam.

"Your body captivates me in every way," said the Persian captain, boldly caressing her thighs, directly beneath her husband's gaze. Let him look, thought the Captain. In this way he will grow more docile. The rooster has been beaten in battle and his spurs are down. We can enjoy ourselves and then give the Macedonians back their cold meat, filled with Persian spices. Such was his contempt, ladies of Athens, and, alas, the wife of the Macedonian chief was responding to his blatant and outrageous advances, fight against them though she would. Perhaps the Macedonian women are less proud that we women of Greece, but I cannot help thinking that it is the same all over. Her husband's honor was already trampled; now her own must follow and in the following she was not completely miserable. For as I said, woman carries in her an urge that is beyond defilement. It rises, regardless of infamy or outrage. And so she was perspiring and growing moist between her legs.

The custom car made a dramatic screeching stop at the curbstone, where Mister Sam was standing.

"Evening, boys," he said. "Out for a little drive, I see."

The boys laughed, speaking only to each other, their voices muted. The grocer went back into the store with a customer. Mister Sam sidled over to the car and gave a comic wiggle of his hips as he leaned against the fender. "There must be a lot of power under *this* hood," he said, raising his eyebrows.

"Want to go for a ride?" asked a voice from the front seat.

"Well," said Mister Sam, "as long as you don't drive too fast."

"Our success in battle is legendary," said the Persian captain. Then in her ear: "Did you also know about our superior bed weapon, madame? As fierce as our arm is in the field, so too is the strength of our prick," he whispered, violating her with the common word. She reddened, drew away, but he held her by the wrist and drew her to him. His fellow conquerors were doing the same, enjoying, some of them, the presence of two and three women. They fancied an orgy was in store, a victory celebration with the victors covered in flesh. But the Macedonian chief had a plan; had Demeter, our great Goddess, whispered it in his ear?

"What crowd do you run with, boys," asked Mister Sam as the car sped up the main drag and quickly left the little town behind.

"Here, man," said one of the boys beside Mister Sam, "suck my dick." He unzipped his fly and displayed a limp penis.

"Well, well, you boys *are* out for a good time," said Mister Sam, looking down at the member.

"Suck it, man," said the boy and roughly grabbed Mister Sam's coiffure, ramming his head down.

"Now, boys," said Mister Sam, "there's no need to be rough. We've got all night and I understand perfectly." He closed his lips around the sacred object, which he adored in all its sizes and shapes. Expertly, he quickly raised it to its true height, and while the boys joked and swore, he bore it away to the back of his throat, closing his cheeks deftly on it, hiding his teeth, all gentleness, for he had no wish to alarm. No, he just wanted to suck happily, feeling the excitement rising in the swollen organ. I am their guide. I take them along life's highway.

"Gentlemen," said the Macedonian chief, "I see that our women please you and I am pleased. How else can a man be certain that his wife is truly graceful, unless he sees her performing her most graceful act with another?

Then he has objectivity, then he can truly appreciate her. And so you, our honored guests, will enlighten us as to the prowess of our wives and the pleasure will be ours." The Macedonian lifted his wine glass, sipped from it, continued. "However, they have already been here some hours, and eaten. They have sweated, they have gotten their fingers greasy, their bodies need a washing, no more than a quick shower, a brief ablution, that they may return to you, radiant, perfumed, in order that you may perform your duty as guests, servicing them happily and long through the night. Are we agreed, Captain?"

"Agreed," said the Persian captain, giving his woman a slap on the rump. "Go frolic in your bubbles, madame, and grow still more eager for your guest's gift, which he shall save for you."

"He sucks good, does he?"

"Yeah, he's a good old cocksucker," said the center of attraction, suddenly letting go of Mister Sam's soft hair which he had unconsciously clung to after his fierce request.

Mister Sam licked up and down and around, then closed again on the delicious hot popsicle, his favorite sweet, which suddenly quivered and exploded and melted, in his mouth.

"Drink it, man!"

There was no need for shouting. Mister Sam got most of his protein this way. With a smile he swallowed the exotic beverage.

The Macedonian women withdrew to their private chambers once more, and there a curious transformation took place. A group of beautiful beardless Macedonian youths had been assembled. They were exquisite elfin creatures, young men who were almost women. Nay, they seemed like some fantastic sex beyond women. I don't have to tell you, ladies. You know how these twilight creatures can beguile with their exaggerated female ways, the deft flirtations of a woman rendered more bold by that spark of masculinity which these girlish boys retain.

With giggling and merriment, they dressed themselves in the gowns the women had worn, and more skillful than any woman they made up their eyes, sequining the lids, shadowing their gaze with hues of amber and blue. No muscles were seen in these arms; they were white as ivory and soft as milk. Yet for all their giggling and teasing, one could detect a furious cunning in their flamboyant eyes.

"I'm next, man."

Mister Sam's head went down again as another dick looked up at him. All sizes and shapes, I love them without thought of race, color, or creed. He closed his mouth happily on the new offering.

"They are returned to you again, men of Persia. Our wives are refreshed and, from what I have gathered from their whispers, they are eager to hurt you with their passion!"

Through the night the car sped, with Mister Sam blowing strong.

"Come to us, then!" shouted the Persian captain, standing drunkenly, for in the absence of the women the only pleasure was more wine and the Persian officers had continued to drink it wildly. The captain sank back down on the cushions with a laugh, his head spinning. His hostess came toward him, more beautiful than he'd remembered her, her body lustrous from her bath, her skin stimulated, no doubt, by rushing water. "Come here, little wife," said the captain, "and rub your perfumes into my beard."

"You're hurting me, young man," said Mister Sam as the boy held him tightly, twisting his arm up behind his back. The car smelled of semen and beer and whiskey and vomit.

"Shut up, you fucking faggot."

"Haven't I treated you boys nicely? Didn't I give you all a good blow job?"

"Toss him out of the mother-fucking car."

"Boys! Please. Don't leave me out here. It's a long way back to town. I'll pay for your gas; just let me get to my wallet." Mister Sam squirmed. It had happened before. He'd been left out on some dark lonely road in the middle of nowhere many times. The young boys are always so fickle after they've been blown.

"You're ready now, are you, madame?" said the captain, running his hand again slowly up the thigh of the beautiful creature beside him, who smiled wickedly, pulled out a dagger and stabbed the captain mortally in the middle of his laughter, as did the other vicious twilight creatures to their Persian suitors, drenching the banquet with waves of blood, and standing then, in profound silence, over the dead bodies.

Mister Sam's head was out the window and the night

air was blowing his careful coiffure all to pieces, flattening out the ringlets, as the wind stung his eyes and took his breath. "Boys!" he yelled. "Boys! I'm . . . your . . . friend!"

The door suddenly swung open and he was out in the night, and bounced on the crushing pavement, and was dead.

10

Artremnesia was a woman not to be scorned. Though a Persian enemy, she was a woman of power, like a goddess of the sea. Yes, ladies, she was a seawoman—the captain of a ship of fighting men in the fleet of mighty Xerxes, and her proud vessel sailed in the attacking fleet against the Greeks. She was a woman leading men into battle and she had the ear of great Xerxes who respected her every word. In her there was a fire like that which is lit at the foot of Demeter's altar, and that fire is love, and her lover was the King of Calyndia, an ally, sailing in the fleet of

Xerxes. Rumor has it that Artremnesia and the Calyndian King had quarreled, and as they entered battle together against the Grecian fleet the quarrel was still unresolved.

"All right, Joyce," said Mr. Woodrow Jones to his wife, "I put the new molding up around the window. Here's a can of wood putty and a little screwdriver. Just dip a dab of putty onto the end of the screwdriver and put it into the nail holes of the molding. It's a nice easy woman's job."

"Thank you, dear," said Mrs. Jones, and taking the can of wood putty she went to work filling the holes. She always did the little jobs around the house.

The spray danced across the ship's bow and Artremnesia stood upon the deck, her hair blowing in the wind, her eyes fixed ahead of her to the approaching Greek fleet, with whom battle would soon begin. When she looked to the side, to the boat which sailed next to hers, she saw the ship of the King of Calyndia and the King himself, in gold helmet, pacing the deck. Their love had been furious and grand, but today that love was no longer, or so her crew thought, for she was sharp with them, and they feared the awful wrath which had come upon her since leaving their last port, the Hellespont, where she and the King had quarreled.

"Okay, Joyce, I finished making the shelves for the bathroom. You can clean up the workbench now."

"Yes, dear," said Mrs. Jones, taking the dustpan and broom. What a mess the man leaves after him, shavings and glue and bent nails. Well, I'm happy to clean up behind him. After all, he did all the hard work.

The ships of the two fleets came closer. Artremnesia had the look of death in her eyes. A more fierce captain one will not find in any fleet, ladies, than this brave woman, cold in her decisions, stunning in her beauty, the kind of woman a king could dare to love.

"Joyce, when you feel like it, there's a little touch-up work you can do on the windowframes. Here's a small brush. I've done the big stuff; I'd rather not waste my time at such a little job. It'll be just right for you. Maybe I'll wash the car."

"Certainly, Woodrow," said Mrs. Jones, taking the little brush and filling in, here and there.

The salt air was on Artremnesia's lips, and an Athenian ship was in position for battle with her. The Athenian warriors could be seen clearly, their weapons glistening, their beards black, their eyes calm, waiting the engagement.

From his ship the King of Calyndia watched the woman captain in her maneuvering with the Athenians. How beautiful she was and how skilled in battle. And he regretted, perhaps, his cruel words to her in port at the Hellespont. He could see her face more clearly with every moment, for her ship had swerved away from the Athenians and was heading directly toward his own ship. Every man aboard the Calyndian ship was suddenly frozen in contemplation of the wild swan-ship that approached them, as if it were completely out of control. Yet its captain could be seen, her fair hair streaming out behind her, her outstretched arm indicating the direction she wished to pursue.

"My King!" cried the Calyndian captain. "She is going to ram us!"

Artremnesia came gloriously onward, the last rays of the dying sun behind her, the fury of the sea in her eyes. The King of Calyndia stood upon the deck of his ship, which was trying vainly to avoid her. He looked, then, directly into her eyes and nodded his head slowly just before she struck, cracking his ship in half.

"Joyce, would you please stop whistling for a while? I'm trying to think through an important plan here for where to build a whatnot shelf in the den. I've got to concentrate. You know, it's brain work."

Artremnesia looked back over her shoulder to where the collision with King Calyndia had been and there was only the churning sea with not a single head bobbing in it.

11

Io, daughter of King Inachus, went with several of her handmaidens to the shores of the waterfront, where a Phoenician ship had docked and strange objects from Asia were for sale. Io was beautiful and the day was lovely with a gentle wind blowing in from the sea. She strolled along the edge of the water, purchasing this and that, one bright object after another, when suddenly a still more brilliant figure caught her eye—that of the Phoenician captain, who stood upon the deck of the ship in silence, his muscular arm extended casually forward, his hand hanging over the edge of the ship's rail. He seemed as distant from her as Asia itself, his eyes staring upward to the hills beyond the shore and she, naturally enough, desired that they be cast upon her own lovely form, for was she not the perfect expression of that land?

Her private chamber in the back room of the Forty-second Street bookstore was a dream world of lust where she showed her big boobs to the world. Buxom is not word enough to describe the enormity of her knockers, rendered all the more enormous-seeming by the fact she was only five foot three in her bare feet. Disrobing in the dressing room, she walked, like the great actress that she was, into the room with the windows and the revolving platform. She was from a nice wholesome middle-class small-town American family; she raised one leg onto the platform and heard the coin-operated window shades being drawn. Immediately her nice wholesome middle-class small-town American hole got wet. How she loved to have them look at her boobs!

He'd come across the sea with treasure and he saw now a treasure he might take back with him. The fair Io had finally caught the captain's attention by holding up a golden egg from Persia, and exclaiming loudly over it with her handmaidens, turning her body so that the sun's rays from beyond the hill passed through her thin gown in such a way that the hills of her breasts became clear to him.

"There are still stranger objects on board," said the captain softly, but his voice carried down to the keenly attentive girl. Ah, ladies of Athens, thus is it always—she must waken him from his sleep, from his dreaming, and teach him of beauty. But he was awake to her now and he sent his cabin boy down to guide her and the handmaidens onto the ship.

Her tits were possibly the largest ever shown on Forty-second Street. They were a fascination to her as well as to the men behind the dark windows. What were such big boomers for, if not to display this way? Sitting naked on the slowly turning platform, she felt the deepest expression of her being. Every woman wants to do this. She turned onto her side, elbow bent on the platform, supporting her head in her hand. Show our boobies. I'm showing my boobies. Look, you hungry bastards, and hang your dongs. They all have their sausages out in my honor. Beyond the windows, which cast back numerous reflections of her white body, pricks were raised. She rolled over on her back, looking at the ceiling, and ran her tongue over her lips. She raised one leg slowly, straight up like a dancer. Some guy is now getting a quarter's worth of look up my smoozey. Maybe he can see how wet it is. I love it, Mommy and Daddy, this I love. And she lowered her right leg and raised the left leg, wriggling her toes.

"Just ahead of you," said the Phoenician captain, "is my cabin. It is there I keep the most precious of curios."

Her maidservants had somehow been separated from her by the eyes and curls of the sailors, no doubt, and she was for the captain. The door of the cabin swung open. Her heart beat wildly. Now that her little egg had been purchased, she had enough. His flirtation was all she wanted, no more, just a frivolous stroll along the beach. But she had not reckoned on the call that all sailors learn from the sea maids of the rocks. Suddenly she was in his wooden room upon the water, seeing her native hills through a tiny round window. "What worlds this window has seen," she said, trying to be as calm as the ocean beneath her.

"No world so alluring as you, girl of the golden egg," he said.

"You have practiced your words," she said.

"Only in preparation for you," he said, and touched her hair, gently twining it on his finger.

She touched herself there, running her hand ever so slowly up along her thigh, until it reached her beaver and she brought it slowly up over her beaver, dragging it through the hairs. The window drapes continued to open and close, first one, then the other. It was a familiar and comforting sound. It beat working at the A & P. She lay in warm light on the Persian carpet and watched the ceiling turn. Her hands came up over her soft belly, and up over her rib cage, and up to her super boobs. She squeezed and caressed them. She was the best show on Forty-second Street; even the manager of the store occasionally took a turn in the booth, watching her. She was into her work and knew all the ups and downs of autoerotic body movement. She rolled over on her stomach and pressed down against the warm carpet, sending a shiver up through her whole body.

I'm hot, so hot, she thought, lifting her sweet rear off

the platform and turning it slowly around in a circle, giving the boys at the back window a shot of her beaver from behind. Her sweet little beaver with its long slit and clitty-nose. You love it, don't you, boys, you'd love to suck on it if I'd let you. But it's so nice in here, all by myself, just like being on television. Their eyes are popping out of their heads; they've already come in their handkerchiefs. Sometimes they make sounds, groaning and growling sounds. Let them grovel. One John comes and licks at the window. I'm the one they love, not their wives or their girlfriends. They go home and fuck their wives and it's me they shoot into me. They see my big boobies swinging and my little toes. I'm so beautiful. I'm the most beautiful thing that ever came out of Echo Lake, New Jersey. None of the sorority clubs would let me in because my boobs were the biggest in the school. But who was voted Most Likely To Succeed In Show Business? Me, Edwina Sutlock, and men adore me.

She heard someone knocking at the glass. She looked up and saw him, his pants down, standing on a chair, his upright dick pressed against the glass. I understand. He wants me to see. She smiled and blew him a kiss, and, as she expected, a second later he shot all over the window. He'd saved it up for her and now he disappeared back into the shadows, and she watched the sperm dripping down the window slowly, his offering at her temple. She hoped he enjoyed it, hoped he'd go home and give his stupid old wife a good screwing.

The captain's hands were upon her and she struggled

for a moment, but fell quickly. We are so weak, ladies of Athens, in this way, while we are so strong in other ways. The feel of his member against her young thighs was overwhelming. She closed her eyes, his ship sailed into her heart, she even cried a bit, quivering naked on his bunk. But he warmed her soon enough with that most exquisite of all curios, made not only in Asia, but in our land too, made everywhere, my dears, that art object fashioned by the Goddess herself for her ultimate pleasure.

She stood, shook her titties a bit. How she loved to feel them there. They were always the best surprise. When she woke up in the morning, there they were, like a miracle. She bowed her legs, stood on tiptoe, and swiveled her pelvis. I'm a little miracle. They crawl out of holes in the wall to see me. I wish they had a toilet in this room, so they could watch me shit. Mother always made me leave the bathroom door open while I went. So I shouldn't do anything dirty to myself in there. Here I am, Mama, your daughter is doing the slow dirty coozie boogey for all the freaks in town.

If they had a toilet I could save my evening shit for them. I'd wipe myself slowly. I'd turn around so they could see me wiping the shit off. Everything—I want them to have everything I can give. They ought to put a shower in, too, then they could watch me wash my sweet tits, foaming them with soap, and soaping up my hole, getting it all soapy and sticking my finger up and making it nice and clean.

Here the distinguished lady of Athens lifted her skirt,

and hugging it above her thighs, showed in a matter-of-fact way, her round mound of coal-black hair. It is a pauper's purse, she said, until the bar of gold is placed inside it. She looked down at the black purse, quizzically, as if trying to fathom the deepest of all Demeter's secrets, that mystery of soft lips where sweet eternity is sung, mystery of mysteries, built by the Goddess in ancient times forever sealed. And then she looked up, laughing, stripping herself completely, as did Io, the captured girl of her tale.

My favorite place in all the world is right in this room, getting myself hot. She curled up on the platform, her hands folded between her legs, like a fetus. She squeezed her legs, pressed her fingers into her smoozey, into the soft wet folds. Slowly she stretched out her legs again and, spreading them apart, began to tickle her clitty, lightly, just the way she liked it, the way nobody else could, stopping just at the right moment and starting again.

She rubbed her hands in the bearded beaver as the window curtains opened and closed. They were all going at it now, pounding their meat with her. Let's all come together, fellas. Oh, I love it so warm in the lights, what else can I do with my boobs, my beaver, my life? I just want to come, honey, all over. She stood up, clutching her pussy, shaking her tits, and then slowly sank down again to the platform, working her finger in and out and laying her thumb gently on the clit. In the bathroom, with the door open and everybody watching, she gave a long sigh and stretched her lovely legs outward, way out, coming in one long bright wave all over Forty-second Street, again and again, with pricks in the air.

Io felt the world swaying; could it be he was such a powerful lover that her whole being was tossed and rocked this way? The boat was sailing, ladies, Io had been abducted. A curio chaser, chasing after a golden egg, she leapt up, naked, severed from all shame, and saw through the porthole her native hills slipping forever behind her.

It is said she was not altogether unhappy, for directly behind her was the captain with a most quiet order which she playfully obeyed. Silly girl! And so, for a child's whim, the Great War began.

King Inachus swore that his daughter had been forcefully carried away, which is no doubt true. But I ask you, ladies, is any woman ever taken completely by force?

12

Great Plutarch has told of Ismenodora, the lovely widow who was enamored of the beautiful young boy, Bacchon. She was wealthy, he a mere cadet of the Palestra where, having sported naked with the other boys, he had gained many admirers. These young men, and not a few old men, adored beautiful Bacchon and wanted to see him naked in their midst. But we know the strength of a woman whose desire has been aroused. Ismenodora wanted the young man, and considered that her breasts, her thighs, her languid loveliness, were as more than a match for the muscles of the gymnasium boys with whom Bacchon played each day.

Officer Slug went into his dressing room and took out his eyeshadow, mascara, and nylon stockings.

Bacchon's manliness was not in question. Ismenodora knew that once he was in her arms, he would discover the true nature of woman and his own true nature would spring up, full-boned and ready. The thought of it filled her night with lonely lubrication, for she had seen Bacchon in the stadium, had seen that untried manhood hanging so ripe, so strong—but crossed by a boy's limbs. Late in the darkness she sighed and wished that she were a man, that she could join in the sport of the Palestra and touch her beloved. But then, touching herself upon the breasts and upon her swelling vulva, she recollected herself and knew that the greater power was still hers, if she could only play it skillfully.

"Officer Slug, are you ready to do your duty?" asked the captain of the vice squad. "Do you have your billy-stick and your pocketbook? I must say you're lookin' lovely tonight."

"Thanks, Cap." And now I go out of the station house to patrol in my high heels and catch some motherfuckin' son of a bitch junkie purse-snatcher. Tits. Wig. Lipstick. It feels kinda nice with my nylons rubbin' back and forth against each other. Give myself a hard-on if I don't watch out. But my dick is strapped down, and tucked beside my European-style unshaved armpits is a .45 revolver. I added a dash of perfume behind my ears, nothin' too strong, just a touch of *Ma Griffe*. What a lovely night to catch a pervert and punch him in the puss. Look at me there, in the reflection of that shop window—sexy? Man, I am hot stuff, cotton-wad tits, and false bra with rubber nipples. Some motherfucker is going to get a surprise tonight, Mr. Mayor. Officer Slug is on duty!

Ismenodora paced in the near darkness of the new moon. She'd seen Bacchon that afternoon, walking past her house in the company of other boys and his beauty shone like love's sword, impaling the hearts of his companions. Bacchon, my darling, my sweet, she whispered out her window to the night. Her period of mourning was over; her husband had died in battle, leaving her with riches and freedom. The elusive boy had caught her resurgent desire. It would be foolish to try and seduce him slowly, she thought, through showing myself here, and there, when he passes. His guard is too shrewd, they cover him in praise and affection, screening him off from the deeper pleasure which only a woman's body can generate in a man. The little wretches, the naked little goat-boys. I'll have to act forcefully to cut through their ranks and spoil their caresses. Oh, moon, how may I enchant him as he has enchanted me?

Yes, I'm lookin' devine tonight, kinda like Sophia Loren with my sequined eyelids. I'm glad I wore the dark wig tonight; it brings out the brown in my eyes. I'll catch me a purse snatcher and ram my billy-stick so far up his asshole his eyes will pop out.

The boys were all that stood between Ismenodora and Bacchon, and with that in mind she arrived at the only conclusion possible. At dawn she summoned her maids and servants and all day they watched at the gates of her house, while she bathed and hummed and selected her most devastating gown. The day was bright, but the night was in her eyes.

Some guy on the corner givin' me the eye. I'll just shake my ass a little. Maybe he'll try to steal my pocketbook. Won't he get a motherfuckin' surprise between the eyes. Come on, big boy, come over here and try to molest me.

He's turnin' into a barroom. You're afraid of a beautiful woman, you creep. Well, I'll just keep walkin'. I'm quite comfortable in high heels. Last week I ran down a purse snatcher in them, chased him five blocks and punched his lights out in a hallway. They can't escape Officer Slug. She's too fast.

Fast are the runners of the Palestra and fast their fingers when they make their coy caresses, but they were not quite so swift as Ismenodora's wit. They thought their prize was safe within their grasp; they feared no rival from outside the gymnasium. Bacchon was to be their sport, their glory, and arm in arm they walked along, after the day's practice, enjoying that rough yet touching tenderness of youth's love of itself. Bacchon was a god! His golden crown of curls danced as he bowed his head to another's shoulder with a laugh that was also the swiftest kiss. Ladies of Athens, it is sad, we must admit, that such loving youths be parted from each other. But if women did not take some action, our heroes would not be born. Thus is Ismenodora justified, and as the boy lovers walked past her gates, her servants ran out and, with surprise their ally, they dragged Bacchon away from his crowd.

Officer Slug, you are the best-lookin' piece of ass on Broadway tonight. There's a hard-lookin' broad in that doorway, but I think my tits are bigger. What is this, she's steppin' out alongside me. Gee, what a sexy voice.

"You're ravishing tonight, my dear."

"Yeah, ya think so?" What is this, what is this, what's this dame drivin' at. If I weren't in this outfit, I'd pick her up, maybe, give her a fast screwin' in the hallway. But I'm on duty. I can't go fuckin' around tonight.

"Simply gorgeous. Why don't you come along with me. I know a swinging party where girls like us can have a good time."

"Sorry, I ain't got the time tonight. I'm—"

"Do you have a date?"

"Yeah . . . yeah, that's it; I've got a date."

"I bet he likes your hairy balls."

"WHAT?"

"Oh, come on, honey, don't be so uptight, we're in the same bag. Your eye makeup is cool, but you've got thighs like a rhinoceros."

"Some men like a muscular calf." I've got to shake this dizzy broad. She's a psycho. I've got to find me a purse snatcher and bash his lights out. I can't waste any more time. "Well, I've got to run along."

"Don't be in such a hurry. I'm telling you, you'd really dig this party. Look, you've got a pair of balls and I've got a pair too, you dig? And I've got some friends all dressed up like us and we can go there. . ."

"TO A PERVERT PARTY?"

"Yeah, baby, that's it, for freaks only."

"Why, goddammit, you must think—I'm some kind of fuckin' pervert!"

"Well, what are you?"

"I'm . . . I'm. . . ."

"You're queer, I'm queer, come on, let's hop in a cab. TAXI!"

I'd better follow this joker. I may actually round up an entire nest of perverts. What a catch for Officer Slug!

Through the iron gates of Ismenodora's courtyard young Bacchon was led, the servant girls showering him with flowers and laurel wreaths, and one of them playing the flute, and Bacchon had to smile, for he knew that no harm would come to him here.

"Nowhere in the world," said Ismenodora to her beloved, "is one so beautiful as you, Bacchon." He was led to her incensed chamber. She lay in a white gown, exceedingly revealing, and the doors closed behind him and he was alone with her, except for the sound of the flute, playing sweetly somewhere below the high open window.

13

Ladies of Athens, Periander's wife died, rather suddenly. Gripped by the nightmare of grief, plunged in loneliness, he sought his relief upon his beloved Melissa's dead body. Yes, my dears, he impregnated the fatal loveliness of his wife. A chilling story, but one favorite to Demeter. Are those of you who removed your gowns feeling cold at the thought of that icy body on which he laid himself? Ladies, my tale will show clear proof of the soul's hidden presence. Yes, Melissa somehow felt the violation, for something of life is contained in death, that compelling statue. The fading rainbow is the reflection of the sun and Periander tried to breach the gulf across eternity, laying himself upon his lifeless wife. How still was the moon of ghosts.

"Play that song again, will you, honey," said the drunken blonde seated at the piano bar. The piano player smiled and played it again and she came and sat next to him on the bench and stuffed a ten-dollar bill in his jacket pocket. "George and I would like you to come to a little party we're having this evening." She nodded toward a bald-headed man, seated further down the piano bar. His drink rested on the shining lid. He smiled and gave a little drunken wave of his fingers.

"Okay," said the piano player, "after I finish my last set."

"Swell, honey, we'll have a fun time. George's loaded, if you like money. Do you like money?"

"Yeah," said the piano player, "I like money."

"Well, you'll make some money tonight, how's that?"

"That's fine."

Periander did this thing, ladies, and lived to think about it. A friend of his asked him for a certain object he had borrowed. Periander looked for it, but could find it nowhere. So he went to the oracle of the River Acheron, where the ghost of his wife appeared unexpectedly. She was cold, she said. The clothes she wore in the grave did not keep her warm.

I am cold, she said. *I need clothes, warm clothes.*

First Periander suspected it was a demon sporting with

him. But then the ghost spoke a curious sentence, which shook his soul to the marrow.

You put your loaves into a cold oven, said the ghost of Melissa.

The temple of the oracle was shadowy, for it is such shadows the dead prefer. She held herself like a wisp of smoke in the cold stone room. *I am cold and need warm clothes. You put your loaves into a cold oven.*

"You play awfully well," said George, as he and his lady friend and the piano player climbed into a taxicab. The cab sped along the empty streets to the East Side of Manhattan, up into the elegant towers, where doormen waited faithfully through the night for the late-crawling dwellers or for an occasional burgler, with whom they were in league.

"He's very talented," said the blonde, running her fingers through the piano player's curly black hair.

The piano player sat, drunk, impervious. During ten years of cocktail piano in New York City, he had tasted all the drinks. He'd tasted them all, but this one was going to be some kind of kick, for the blonde was obviously into George for clothes and stones. It could be like one good night of poker where you come away rich. Well, I'll poke her, or George, or their fuckin' rubber plant, if it comes to that. New York.

Periander was shocked to the roots of his hair. The dead feel and hear; the dead speak when they are spoken to. And he felt again the dead body all around him; even as he walked into the street, he felt the impress of the dead flesh, so cold and bare, the picked flower going limp in his arms. How terrible to have this deathly crime on my soul.

"Make Melissa an offering to alleviate her chill," the oracle said.

The moon worked its way through the night smog, illuminating George's penthouse apartment. They stood in the dark for a few moments, and the piano player felt on his trousers, a hand, fiddling with his crotch.

"There," said George, switching on a light, "that's better." A red bulb, concealed within a potted plant, made the room look like a subdued heart, faintly glowing, casting strange shadows of irregular jungle leaves upon the walls.

"Here's the bar," said George, rolling it out and opening it up. George was a short, round-headed man with fat cheeks and sensual lips. Upon the walls were many paintings.

"All gather round!" The Corinthian street crier rang his gong. "All gather round!"

The people of the town gathered to him, the women standing in curious groups, whispering to each other, the men holding themselves quiet and tense. The crier claimed to bear a message from the father of the city, Periander the Chief, Periander the Great Warrior.

"All women," said the crier, "are to strip naked. This is to begin at once."

The excitement was tremendous. Several young girls who'd had no attention that day were the first to throw their clothes away. Orders are orders; a proclamation from on high mustn't be disobeyed. It was nothing short of a disgrace to continue standing around with one's clothes on. Other women were forced to strip by the soldiers and soon the clothes became a pile heaped in the middle of town, as woman after woman came, naked and bearing her gown in her arms. The gay mood was not in the crowd though, for they sensed something awesome was behind the strange request. Even the boldest of the soldiers remained no more than a servant, assisting the women as they laid stitch after stitch of clothing on the growing pile.

"Well, I'm going to make myself comfortable," said the blonde, shaking out her long hair. "Does anybody mind?" She unbuttoned her dress and stepped out of it. Her brassiere was transparent, with black hands embroidered on it. "A present from George."

"I like sparkle," said George, stirring the drinks.

The piano player blinked again. On the blonde's panties were flirtatious, winking eyes. Her legs were long, her stockings decorated with sheer butterflies. She flopped in a chair, a drink in her hand and said, "He likes money, George."

"Yes, of course," said George, "who doesn't? Fortunately I have a great deal of money. Here," he said, opening his wallet, and handed two five-hundred-dollar bills to the piano player, who slipped the bills into his pocket. "Would you like to see the bedroom?" asked George, leading the way into a dark room, which quickly became red. The bed was kingsize, and the woman stretched out upon it.

"George would like you to undress me now," she said. "Isn't that right, George?"

"Yes," said George, "we're among friends."

The piano player removed his jacket, tossed it over a chair, and sat on the bed beside the woman.

It was near the end of day. The pile grew, bigger and bigger, with gowns and frocks and underpinnings. Out of the dark gloom of the twilit buildings, Periander stepped. His armor was bronze, with the breast-plates of a lion. His sword weighed heavily in the land, and flanked by his soldiers, he stood, eyes narrowed in concentration, watching the pile of clothing grow in the night. Like a ghost, white in the darkness, it rose, and he could hear Melissa whispering in the dark, *I am cold. Warm me, my husband.*

"Rub my tits a little. George likes that."

"Yes, I'm very fond of foreplay," said George, seating himself in a nearby chair.

The piano player placed his hands on the embroidered hands of her bra, and squeezed her breasts.

"Oh, George," said the blonde, sighing, "you're so naughty."

"I can't help myself," said George from his chair. "I was born fast."

When the clothes were piled high in the night, and every woman in town was naked in the moonlight, Periander strode slowly over to the pile. "Bring me fire," he said, for he heard his dead wife Melissa whispering, *I'm cold, my husband, because of loaves inside a cold oven!*

The eyes upon the blonde's panties closed as the piano player rolled the panties off her buttocks and down her thighs, over her knees and down to her ankles where she kicked them off. George, lifting his hand, caught them, and pressed them to his nose, like a woman who dreams inside a scented handkerchief.

The blonde's patch was tinged reddish in the red room. The piano player removed his pants and shirt.

"Strip all the way," said the blonde. "George insists."

"Yes," said George, "I won't be held back."

The piano player was naked in the red light and the blonde was naked, too, except for her stockings and gold high-heeled shoes. "Come on," she said, holding her arms out to the piano player, and drawing him on top of her.

"This is how I like it," said George, opening up his fly and taking out his flaccid member. "Just plain old-fashioned sex."

"Give it to me," said the blonde. "Give it to me, George."

"Yes, I'll give it to you, dear," said George, whacking off in his chair. "Do you feel it going in?"

"Yes," she said, "I feel it going way up inside."

"I've been going to a Chinese doctor," said George.

The fire reflected on the bronze armor. Periander lowered his torch to the pile of feminity, to the gowns and cloaks, the scarves, underthings, which singed, then sang with fire, the silk catching brightly, tossing tongues into the air, so the fire became a great glow in the center of the town.

Periander knelt at the blaze with head bowed and

Melissa spoke from the warmth he'd brought her. *Now, my faithful lover, we have become one again in the dark fire. Now I can appreciate that last caress you gave me from afar. I am feeling alive again in the warmth of your offering. And if you wish for proof that I was really here, then go to the house of Plotinous, and there, in the corner beside his wooden lampbox, you will find an object of which you had forgotten the whereabouts.*

Periander went to the appointed house, and indeed he did find, as the ghost had said he would, a carved bronze phoenix rising from a pedestal of flame.

"This is a weird scene, baby," whispered the piano player to the blonde, as he stroked her.

"You love it," said the blonde.

"Yes," said George, stroking his own bone, "I like nothing better than a good screw."

14

I will tell you about Melonisia, the lady who loved geometry. Her cheeks were the moon but her mind was on the stars. "She who loveth the stars cannot love man," so they say, and Melonisia knew the secret of the moon's eclipse, for she had studied the wheel of the heavens.

"AGNES!"

A deep voice boomed out in the courtyard of the tenement building on One hundred first Street, off Riverside Drive. There was an empty moment, and the voice called again, tremendous, shaking the windows of the building:

"AGNES!"

"Whatchoo want, honey?" A soft sweet voice came out of a window, dripping honey down the airshaft.

"AGNES, GETCHOO BLACK ASS DOWN HERE!"

Melonisia walked alone from her geometry class through the darkness of the warm night. In her head was a great secret, known only to the learned mathematicians—the moon would fade into a dark shadow tonight, and would be gone, wiped out from the sky. Now the sky over Melonisia held a moon full and in splendor, a lover's moon, perhaps, but soon it would fade into obscurity and love would tremble.

"YOU GETCHOO BLACK ASS DOWN HERE FO' AH COME UP AND KICK IT DOWN HERE!"

"Now just wait a minute, honey." Sweet chocolate-cherry words dripped down the airshaft.

"AH AIN'T GONNA WAIT LONG," grumbled the voice on the street below, muttering like a tank rolling over a rock pile.

Melonisia knew the moon and the moon knew Melonisia, for she shined upon her a pale lovely light which attracted a wandering necromancer, the kind of man who is learned in the stars and is said by some to even travel to the stars. He was struck by the girl, moon-going herself through the darkness without fear. He was handsome with black mustache and glittering eyes. "I have a secret from the gods," he said to her.

"AGNES? AH'M COMIN' UP WIF A GUN IF YO' DON'T GET YO' ASS DOWN HERE!"

"You ain't got no gun, darlin', to speak of."

"AH GOT A GODDAMN GUN AH GON' SHOVE UP YO' BLACK ASS IN 'BOUT FIVE SECONDS, AGNES!"

"Oh, honey, you so baaaad!"

"A secret of the stars," said the necromancer, "which I shall give to you."

They were on the avenue of rare and dark dreams. The sky held a secret what secret?

"I shall perform a piece of magic for you," said the necromancer, "a thing not easily done." He came closer to her in the shadows. She held to her own dignified footstep for she too knew a secret, a thing not easily known, which the geometrists had shown her, that the moon would go out soon this night. What does this man know of the night?

"I cannot always perform this. I can never perform it alone," said the necromancer. "But I can perform it with a beautiful woman in the cool of the evening when the moon is at her fullest ambition as on a night like tonight."

His gaze was dazzling like the moon itself. Is it a lover's fervor? Has he been drawn to me by the moon? The night of stars is an enchanted lagoon so they say.

"But where, sir, will you perform your magical feat?" she asked.

"Where we are sitting," he said. "I am now in perfect correspondence with the moon."

"AGNES! AH'M COMIN' UP TO WHIP YO' BLACK ASS. AH GOT MAH FOOTS ON DE FUST STAIR!"

A policeman walked down One hundred first Street and, hearing the tremendous voice that was booming there, looked in the courtyard of the building. He was reassured that all was well when he saw only a small black man, about five feet tall, calling up the airshaft.

"AGNES? AH'M GONNA COUNT THREE! YO' HEAR ME? YO' AIN'T DOWN HERE BY TIME AH COUNT THREE, AH'M GONNA BREAK YO' DOOR DOWN!"

The policeman walked on.

"The moon, madame, and I, hold a secret trust," said the necromancer, and gesturing toward the heavens, he spoke to the night's jewel: "Dame of the Moon, Crystal Empress, I ask in behalf of this rare lady that you perform with me a most wondrous feat!"

The night was vast and spread out around him. How lonely Melonisia felt in its great and ponderous embrace stretching out black into everlasting distances. She quivered at the sight of the necromancer in black with his strange eyes, marked by wizardry. She dallied, seating herself upon a large stone in the moonlight. His dark figure appealed to her, so extraordinarily romantic in his black cloak, and bearing beneath his arm, a white skull.

"AGNES? HERE AH COME TO KICK YO' BLACK ASS UPSIDE YO EYEBALLS!"

"Oh, moon, you know of my intentions. I see you in this Athenian woman's face. Shall we show her how precise her correspondence is with us, that she is meant to be here tonight, meant to see a rare celestial show?" He came toward Melonisia, bowed before her. "I can only do this through you. Accept this as a secret gesture of love. It is not a thing I give lightly, for I am incorporating myself with the power of darkness, for the sake of you."

What lover brings such a wondrous gift? she wondered. The necromancer's dancing hand, long and slender, gestured to the night sky.

"AGNES? AH'M GOIN' COUNT TO THREE ONE MO' ONCE!"

"Then, moon, through the power of love and love only is this thing done," said the necromancer, making mysterious movements with the white skull he held in his hand. The skull shone in the moonlight like a smaller moon, a moon in correspondence. Now their eyes corresponded. "I shall veil the moon for you, beautiful one. I reach out to the stars, I grab the fine silken threads of space in my hands and I pull the darkness. . . ."

By her own calculation she knew that this effect was to come about, knew its precise moment, for she too had knowledge of the moon.

"AGNES! AH'M GON' LEAVE MAH FOOTPRINT ON YO' ASS!"

"Ah'll jist be a few mo' minutes, darlin'."

"WHO YO' UP DERE WIF? YO' GOT SOMEBODY UP DERE WIF YO'? AH'M GON' KICK HIS ASS TOO!"

Dark night going over slow and mysteriously, spreading darkness across the face of the moon. . . .

"The moon is gone," said the necromancer, pointing to the darkened sky. "For your beauty has eclipsed it," he said, touching her where her own twin moons were hidden. Melonisia did not draw back from the necromancer's hands. He stood in the shadows, by the rock where she sat, and toyed with her in the darkness of her gown.

"AGNES? AH'M COMIN UP TO KICK DE MOTHAHFUCKIN' ASS OFF YO' AN' ANYBODY ELSE AH FIND YO' WIF. YO' BETTER HIDE HIS ASS."

"Ain't noboby here but me, darlin'. Ah'm jest puttin' on my eye makeup."

"AH'M GONNA GIB YO' SOME EYE MAKEUP! DRIVE MAH FIST INTO DE BACK OB YO' HAID!"

"I had the moon inside me. I gave it to you," said the necromancer, bringing her down from the rock to the soft grass at his feet, bringing her gently, with a hand fine enough to grasp and wield the curtain of the night. Yes, it was common knowledge that the moon would be eclipsed. Yes, she'd known it too; it had been her proud early secret of the night, learned at the university.

At first I thought to expose him, because he was a charlatan. But then he made his gesture to the sky . . . I thought perhaps that all the geometry and calculations of the astrologers were merely confirming what was to be a well-known thing in romance, that a necromancer would veil the moon for me tonight.

"AGNES? AH'M GOIN' UP TO DE BAR FO' A WHILE. DEN AH'M COMIN' BACK DOWN HEAH AN' KICK YOU BLACK ASS GOOD!"

Such is the way a woman's mind works, ladies of Athens, even when it is university-trained.

"AH'M GONNA HAB FIFTY-LEBBEN DRINKS AN' DEN KILL SOMEBODY, AGNES."

15

Ah, ladies, said the next speaker, let us not forget Father Homer, and his tale of Aphrodite and Ares who were so enamored of each other that they screwed at every occasion, whenever Aphrodite's husband, Lord Hephaistos, was away. Lord Hephaistos was no fool and, suspecting his wife of the worst, he contrived to make a trap in which to catch the lovers. A blacksmith by profession, he hammered together a fantastic net of fine steel, which he strung above Aphrodite's bed. Then, with the excuse that he was going off for a few days' vacation, he left his wife to her desires, and, indeed, she quickly summoned Ares to her bed.

"My darling," she said, "let us fuck now, while we may."

"Quite," said Ares, and he flung off her gown and mounted her. No sooner had they begun to shake the bed with their enjoyment, than the subtle snares of the trap fell on them, enclosing them on the bed, joined together, like a pair of dogs.

Officer Slug, in drag, drew his .45 revolver out of his unshaved European women's liberation armpit, and pointing it at the host of the party, said, "All right, stick 'em up."

"Now, Mary," said the host, who was dressed as Wonder Woman, "put that dildo away."

"STICK 'EM UP, YOU PERKVERTS!" cried Officer Slug, tongued-tied with excitement, waving his gun around.

"You have betrayed me!" cried Lord Hephaistos.

"Please, darling," said Aphrodite, "don't make a dreadful scene."

"This party is rapidly turning into a bore, and I don't mean up my ass," said a young man dressed as Martha Washington, heading for the door, only to be stopped by a loud explosion from Officer Slug's revolver, as a whining bullet embedded itself in the doorframe.

The guests instantly froze, knowing they were dealing with a pervert of the first water.

All of the gods came to watch the entanglement of Ares and Aphrodite, and great Hermes said he would give anything to be trapped upon such loveliness. Lord Hephaistos steamed and snorted.

Officer Slug dialed *O* on the telephone. "Get me the police," he said.

"My god, this is right out of Fellini," said a young man who'd been having hormone injections all season, ballooning his titties for the party.

Not until great Poseidon, the sea god, came and promised to give Lord Hephaistos back full payment of everything the Lord had given Aphrodite as her marriage gift did Hephaistos agree to lift his vicious net.

"Hello, Captain, this is Officer Slug speakin'. Send a squad car to 125 Christopher Street, apartment twenty-two, I've got a gang of perkverts cornered." One of the guests, dressed as Earth Mother and wearing five pairs of falsies down his chest, snuck up behind Officer Slug and threw a gold lamé gown over the brave policeman's head. The girls started running out the door and windows. Officer Slug went wild, and fired a shot through the wall screaming;

"EVERY ONE OF YOU PERKVERTS IS UNDER ARREST!" He struggled to get the gown off his head. The apartment had been instantly vacated except for two young men dressed as nuns. Their long habits tripped them up and slowed them down. Officer Slug was at the door before them, barring it with his falsies and .45.

"One false move," he said in a snarl, "and you're dead."

"Fucked again, darling," said one of the nuns with a sigh to his partner, who knelt down on the floor and screamed hysterically, afraid of a front-page story in the

Daily News, to which his mother, in Illinois, subscribed.

Great Ares, rather embarrassed, withdrew his engorged member while the gods stood around and joked (the blushing goddesses had all stayed home).

The two nuns and Officer Slug waited for the squad car. When the assisting detectives came to the door, Officer Slug said, "Watch your step, boys, I've corned a couple of dangerous perkverts."

The nuns were led weeping down the stairs in their habits, and taken in the squad car to the station house, where they spent the night in a cell, recalling visions of monastery life and a filthy limerick about a monk who blew a fart out the window, after which they blew the several other young men who shared the cell with them.

Aphrodite, unruffled, finally stirred and took herself to Cypros, to her lovely altar, where she bathed herself, singing a sweetly satisfied tune. One may trap the goddess, ladies, but we cannot embarrass her in that act which comes to her most naturally.

On the following day, the nuns were bailed out by members of the Gay Liberation Party. On the way from the station house, they were seen by an old woman of the neighborhood, who blessed herself and murmured a silent prayer.

16

The next speaker introduced herself. She was a petite creature, with long blonde hair and a mischievous look in her eye. Her voice was deep and soft and came forth from wet sensual lips.

Well, ladies, I won't try to hide that which you already know—that before I married my husband, I was merely a bathing-house girl.

"Next. Are you next, sir?"

"Why, yes I am," said the eager customer at the Broadway Massage Parlor.

"Just step through there, sir," said the receptionist, "and take your pants off. An attendant will be right with you."

"Thank you." Get my carrot whacked, three dollars. Best deal in town. Buy of a lifetime. Probably go nuts without it, after a hard day at the office. Good for the soul, good for the economy. Five dollars a blow job. Can't afford that, I've got to pick up a pizza for the wife and kids on the way home. Only enough money for a hand job to take away the day's tension.

All the men in the city came to the baths and I, clad in a loose toga, washed them all over and so became knowledgeable about their most private parts.

"Good evening," said the attendant, entering the room. She wore a tight-fitting skirt and a rubber vest, had dyed blonde hair, excessive eye makeup, and went straight to her customer, taking hold of his suddenly pulsing pecker.

I have a good memory for details and I can tell you the shape of your own husband's member. But don't be jealous, ladies, I beg you, for never was there anything between us but a little soap and water. Of course, they insisted on being well rubbed and cleaned in certain places so that they might be sweet-smelling for you when they came home at night.

"Nice day, isn't it?" she asked, slowly pulling the foreskin up and down.

"Lovely," said her customer.

"I'm working my way through acting school," she said, taking his beating boner between her two hands and rubbing it back and forth.

"Everyone should express themselves."

"Yes, I want to be creative. Do you know anybody in show business?"

"Well, I meet quite a few actors. I work at the unemployment office around the corner."

"It's such a hard field to crack," she said, expertly working the customer's dong up and down, neither too fast nor too slow.

For the pleasure of our Goddess, and your stimulation, I shall attempt to describe a few of the outstanding pricks in Athens. First there is Lucian, whose member must be excruciatingly long when it is erect. I, of course, have only seen it hanging passively in the bath.

"You must see a lot of cocks in a day," said her customer.

"Yes, I do. I can tickle your balls if you like, for fifty cents extra."

"Please," said the customer, handing her two quarters, one for each gonad. It would have to be pizza without the anchovies tonight.

"A girl has to make a living," said the attendent, pocketing the two quarters.

"We're all in the same boat," said the customer, groaning and lying backward on the massage table.

. . . and then, ladies, there is Charmides, with his charming tool.

"I'm learning a new scene now. My director has me playing a tree."

"Is that so?" Jisom boner cocky. Chicks warm fucky coozey.

"It feels like you're coming."

"Don't stop, please."

"Oh, don't worry about that. I'm hired to produce a satisfactory ejaculation in any healthy . . . oh, there it goes, isn't it wonderful, you're shooting all over my rubber vest."

"Arrrrrgggghhhhhhh."

"This is the part I truly like, when the coming takes place. It's sort of—primal theater, you know what I mean? I mean, it's so basic."

"Gaaaarrrrrgggggghhhhhhhh."

Of course, I merely soaped it for him, and shampooed his hair. There wasn't the slightest excitation between us, you know that, don't you?

"And sometimes I get such terrific feelings when it happens, all warm sensations and I know it's valuable material for my career. There, that's the last drop."

"There's a little more coming up right behind it."

"It will cost three dollars more if you want me to produce a second ejaculation, sir."

"Do it, here." He handed her his last three dollars. It would have to be a can of sardines and a package of crackers for dinner.

17

Lovely Leukippe then rose amongst the gathered women, and began her tale.

You may remember that I once loved a boy named Tatios. Mother and I came to stay at the house of Tatio's father during the war. Immediately I saw that this boy's eyes were upon me, and it was not long before we had traded kisses. He urged me for more, for a deeper token, for an exchange of passion that would seal us together forever. I must admit it sounded agreeable, but Mother had posted a heavy guard at the door, for she suspected that we would try and do what young people always try to do. But we bribed the maid and drugged the guard and in the night there was Tatios, in my bedroom, and me all aflutter. We lay ourselves down together. Suddenly there was a knock at the door.

"Just relax," said the girl, "it will be all right."

"I can't relax," said the young man. "How can I relax?"

"We'll work it out together, and we'll do whatever we have to do to give you a hard-on," said the girl.

"I'll never be able to get a hard-on with a woman."

"Yes, you will," she said. She was a beautiful actress from the roadshow, and he a young leading man with a sexual problem in that he liked to lead young men into his asshole.

The door opened.

"We are discovered," cried Tatios, and fearing for his life, he leapt from the oven of my desire and made straight for the window, hopping through it, into the night, just before my mother burst into the room.

"Daughter!" she cried. "Are you all right?"

"Yes, Mother," I said, "what is the matter?"

"I had a dream, daughter, that a robber came into your room. He brandished a naked sword, threw you down on your back, and then ripped you up the middle of the belly with his blade. I woke in a cold fright and came straight to you."

The telephone rang.

"Jesus Christ," moaned the actress, her lips around his cock.

"I have to answer it," said the young leading man. "It

might be the director." Mental health is one thing, but show business is everything. "Hello?"

"Hello, Anthony, is that you? Anthony, can you hear me? I'm calling long-distance."

He heard the crackling nagging love-hated insane voice of his mother, far distant, chasing him, following him, TELEPHONING ME NOW, NOW!

"What is it, Mother? How did you get my phone number?"

"I had to telephone the theater. You remember you gave me a list of the theaters you were playing in. I told them it was your mother, that it was an emergency."

His heart sank, along with his hard-on. "What is it, Mother? What's the emergency?"

"There's no emergency, Anthony. I just had to talk to you. I had to hear your voice. I carried you inside me, Anthony. I have a right to talk to you."

"Mother. . . ." His voice choked. There was a ball of hot iron stuck in his throat. There was a fist of burning steel clamping on his balls.

"Do you . . . still love your mother, Anthony, who carried you inside her?"

"Mother, I have to hang up now," he said. "I have a rehearsal in five minutes."

"Oh, Anthony, please phone me back soon. I had the strangest feeling just before I called you. I was just sitting in front of the TV and suddenly I knew I had to call you. It just hit me, five minutes ago. Are you all right, my baby?"

"Yes, Mother, I'm wonderful," he said. The actress brought her head back into his lap and resumed sucking his cock again, and he hung up the telephone and continued the rehearsal.

So there you have it, ladies. The intensity of our passion was felt through the house of Tatios, and invaded Mother's sleep and I was spared that cruel and delightful death at the end of the sword of my lover.

18

The next speaker was a dark-haired beauty, somewhat on the plump side, with a pouting almost piggish face, which accentuated her sensuous nature. Ladies of Athens, she said, I must tell you about a most unfortunate young man, poor Simylos, who was dealt with most terribly by his father.

Dressed in his new custom-made suit, carrying his new briefcase, the young man entered the Seventh Avenue showroom.

Simylos was a lover born, with beautiful features and a

fierce desire. He chased many women and he drank and gave away presents from his father's house. His father was distraught with the young man's licentiousness, and feared that the boy would fritter and fuck away all the family ownings.

"Good morning, Mr. Greenfield," said the receptionist.

"Good morning," said the young man, strolling easily down the corridor.

About this time a friend of Simylos's father suggested that the boy be gelded. "After all," said the friend, "one does not hesitate in gelding a randy animal. I know a fellow who can perform the operation faultlessly, and your son will be healthy as can be a few minutes after it, with just a bit of pitch-ointment on the wounds."

The father had to admit it was a good idea. With his son settled down, they would go into business together and the family name could continue to prosper. At the rate the lad was going now, with all his whoring and drinking, he was bound to come to a bad end. Better to cut his balls off and have done with it—that's the way to make a good business partner out of your son.

"Good morning, Mr. Greenfield," said his secretary as he opened the door to his office, marked:

J. Greenfield, Jr.
Vice President

"Is Dad in yet?"

"He said to tell you he wants you to join him in conference at ten o'clock."

The gelding surgeon was sent for, and arrived with his knives and ointments, in the night, when Simylos was out. Father and surgeon waited in the shadows, until late, when Simylos finally returned, drunk and singing. As he fumbled with his latch key, they grabbed him.

"What is this?" cried the young man.

"My son," said the father, "it is for your own good."

"Yes, please," said the boy, reassured now that he saw it was his own father and not a thief. "I do need some guidance in getting to my bed. I've had a few drops of wine."

"Yes, my boy, right this way," said the father, and he and the surgeon conducted the young man to his bed, where they laid him down gently and then quickly tied him, securing his arms and legs to the bedposts.

"Very good, thank you," said the young man, going past his secretary to his inner office, where he opened his empty briefcase. Soon it would be filled with the numerous memos and letterheads and brochures and correspondence that make for a high-level executive. My career is just beginning; it's a wonderful feeling.

"Dear Father," asked the boy, "what are you doing?"

"This won't take long, young man," said the surgeon. "Just lie quietly."

"Father!" cried the young man. "What are your intentions?" He saw the sudden gleam of a scalpel. It was thin and sharp and the surgeon tested its edge against a fine thread, through which it smoothly passed.

"Now, my boy," said the father, "just be manly and do not flinch. We are going to perform a small operation, the merest touch of the blade. You'll be fit as can be in no time." And so saying the father lifted the young man's gown, so that his private parts were exposed.

"Father!" screamed Simylos. "Please don't, whatever you have in mind!"

"Hush, my lad," said the father. "It's for the good of your soul and our business."

His desk was empty of papers and the drawers were empty too, except for pencils, paperclips, and other accessories. He swiveled his chair around and stared out the window. Yesterday a college graduate, today a vice president. This is the life.

"Hold his thighs open, will you," said the surgeon.

"Help!" screamed the young man. "Someone help me!"

"We are helping you, son. We are doing this for your own good. You'll thank me for it later on."

"No! Father, no, no, no!" screeched Simylos. "This must not be, I am dreaming—!"

"Your idle dreaming is done, dear Simylos," said the father, as the surgeon's knife made its first cut. "Now it's down to business."

Yes, sir, Dad and I will make the business grow together. The sky is the limit. How many fellows my age have their name on the door, and their own secretary? Yes, sir, I've got the world by the balls.

"Father!" screamed the young man once again, before he fainted away. When he woke, it was to the smell of pitch ointment.

19

A willowy blonde rose from the crowd of Athenian women. The top of her gown was loose, and her breasts, small and shapely as the pears of early summer, were almost completely revealed. Ladies, she said, look what I have brought for your entertainment. They were made especially for me by the masterful woodcutter at the gates of our city. Well, you can see—there are two lovely dolls in my hands, a little boy doll and a little girl doll.

"Come in, son," said John Greenfield, Sr., president of Dolls, Inc.,, which had created such million-dollar doll sensations as Baby Tinkle and Patsy Puberty.

The dolls were passed around. The women began to giggle and play with the dolls, which were of a curious kind.

"How're you today, Dad?" asked Vice-president John Greenfield, Jr.

"Fine, just fine, son. I wanted to brief you on our plans for this year's new doll."

"Dad, I have a suggestion."

"Good, good! What is it, my boy?"

"I think we should go more realistic with our dolls."

A frown crossed the brow of the elder Greenfield. "Realistic?"

"Yes, Dad, I've got an idea for a new little-boy doll, with a penis and testicles on it."

"Balls on a doll? You must be crazy, son."

"No, Dad, I'm serious. The public is ready for this kind of doll. I made a few sketches in my office awhile ago. . . ."

"Forget it," said the elder Greenfield. "We're only interested in creating a little playmate for Baby Tinkle. I've got the engineers working on it right now. This name probably won't stick, but right now I call it Baby Kucky. We're working on a lifelike little turd tablet."

Look, ladies, said one of the Athenian women, smiling as she held the little-girl doll in her hand. She has a tiny crack carved in her crotch, and it's lined with a soft spongy material from the sea.

Yes, said another of the lovely ladies, holding the little-boy doll. And *he* has a tiny prick of wood. Isn't it sweet, the way it's sticking up.

"Dad, don't you think there's something misleading

about Baby Tinkle wetting her diaper out of a little metal hole in the middle of her back?"

"It's as good a place as any," said Greenfield, Sr. "Better than most places. No good if it came out of her elbow."

"How about designing a real vagina?"

"A real what?"

"A girl's sexual parts," said Greenfield, Jr., lowering his voice.

"Is that what you learned in college?"

"Dad, I'm a creative person."

"Bullshit, we're in business. Balls on a doll, you must be dreaming, boy. Look at Patsy Puberty. We only barely got away with putting"—Mr. Greenfield looked around to see if his secretary was near—"putting knockers on Patsy Puberty. No nipples, of course. That was the one condition the department stores insisted on. No nipples on Patsy Puberty."

Yes, ladies, said the owner of the dolls, now you are getting the idea—the dolls are meant to fit together in the most intimate fashion. Aren't they the loveliest toys you ever saw?

The Athenian women put the dolls in various positions of love-making, and because the dollmaker had skillfully wired the arms and legs, quite unusual postures were achieved with the toys. Finally, in a tender embrace, little girl straddling the little boy, they were laid on the altar of Demeter.

The ladies all insisted on the name of the dollmaker. This was just the sort of toy they would like to get for their own children. Children need something to occupy their time, and here were dolls that educated them to the ways of love.

"Dad, I want to bring new blood into the business."

"New blood, okay, balls and nipples, no. Cut those balls right out of your mind, my boy, I know what the public wants. It wants Baby Tinkle with a hole in the middle of her back and Baby Kucky with a hole in the same place."

"A doll that shits out of her back?"

"That's right, son. We don't want children to get the wrong idea."

20

I think, ladies of Athens, said the next speaker, that the time has come for us to determine whose bottom is softest, and most sweetly formed. It is the custom every year at our little celebration to chose a championship ass and I have been preparing all year for the prize.

"All right, girls, this way. Please, Miss Arkansas, get into line." Miss Arkansas and Miss Kansas stepped into the Certification Room. It was filled with high-level executives of the Miss Cosmos Pageant. One of them carried a tape measure.

Observe, ladies of Athens, as I loosen my gown. You can see the sweet cheeks of my rump clearly now as I shake them to and fro. Look, they jiggle about so. Can't you see your husbands gaping after such a display? Do you think I'm dangerous? Have I won the show?

"Take off your clothes, girls," said the chairman of the Selection Board. Last year some bitch in an air-inflated brassiere had practically wrecked the show. Luckily, she was detected while having her Miss Alaska banner pinned on her blown-up bosom.

No, by heaven, you have not! cried beautiful Thyrallis, who immediately stood and, not wishing to keep anything hidden from the eyes of the mortals and immortals gathered at the temple of Demeter, quickly stripped off her gown. She turned slowly, so all could see her white round can. Then she drew the cheeks in, puckering them together, saying, Look how beautifully shaped they are, and observe their perfect shade of pale smooth pink. And look how they flow out into my lovely hips, which are neither too heavy nor too lean, but just right, and look here, at the dimples above, on the crown of my rump. And though my cheeks are perfectly shaped, they know how to vibrate, too!

The girls stripped down to their bra and panties.

"All the way, girls," said the chairman.

"All the way?" gasped Miss Arkansas.

"A security precaution."

And so saying, the charming girl caused her ass cheeks to define several magnificent circles in the air, and then she set them all ajiggling up, down, and around as she pleased, causing the women of Athens to lose their breath, and as they regained it with one voice they declared her, in the name of Demeter, to have the loveliest rump in Greece.

Miss Arkansas removed her bra and panties. She would like to have protested, and would have if she had had a better Entertainment Category, but her act was somewhat weak, being an arrangement of "Tea for Two" which she played on the top of her head with silver-plated spoons, changing the pitch of the notes by opening and closing her mouth.

21

I don't have to describe for you the statue of Priapos which sits majestically in the square of our noble city. The God is there, you have seen him many times, stony-bearded with a prick of stone that rises up in marvelous erection.

She opened the mailbox and found a card in it which said:

> *The New York City Post Office, Christopher Street Branch, requests that you appear at window 5. Parcel too big for box.*

You know its every inch, for you have prayed beneath it, that fertility might descend on you. You have stroked its stone head and kissed its cold veins.

She walked down the street, turned over the card, and received from the postman a plain brown-wrapped parcel, marked only with her name. With pounding heart she took it toward home, for she knew its contents. Going quickly to her apartment, she unwrapped the package and there, before her eyes, was her very own:

Relax-a-Finger

a long bullet-shaped instrument. Instructions came out of the box. She opened them and read:

> *This is your cordless, perfectly safe vibrating finger, suitable for facial and foot massage to take away wrinkles and relax tired areas. Insert batteries at rear end, as indicated. Press On switch. Your vibrator is ready to give you delicate soothing relief of tension. Seven inches long.*

Ladies of Athens, just the other night I saw a young woman—I will not name her for perhaps she is with us here tonight—I saw this young woman approach the statue of Priapos. I was hidden nearby, having myself just paid a faithful visit to the erect God. Well, I watched this young vixen go up to the statue and she began to speak to it sweetly, stroking the tremendous prick and calling it *darling* and *lover* and so forth.

She slipped the batteries into the vibrator and turned it on. It filled her hand with a tingling sensation and following instructions she applied it to her cheeks and throat and feet. Then she lifted up her dress, pulled down her panties, and shoved it up her smooze.

She kissed it, ladies, and then she did something unusual, or perhaps it will not seem unusual to you. *I* found it rather strange when the young woman hoisted up her skirt, climbed on the statue, and lowered herself right onto the prick of stone.

"Ah," she sighed, as the friendly Relax-a-Finger engaged her little clitty. She lubricated all over the finger and soon was able to move it deep into herself, so that the very tip of it was vibrating far up in her pie, only the very bottom of it still remaining in her fingertips.

She began to ride the statue, ladies, up and down, sinking the stone shaft deep into herself. You know how smooth the cock in the square is, worn smooth by countless lips and perhaps some other maidens have lubricated it too, as this wench did, raising herself up and letting herself down, so now the shaft appeared and now it disappeared between her legs, traveling heaven knows how far into her.

"Oh, god, I can't stand it," she moaned, circling the Relax-a-Finger round and round and going bowlegged to the couch with it up her, and there she sprawled out, opening her legs wide, lifting her knees up and hump-squirming hungrily.

For fully an hour she entertained the God this way, until quivering, she screamed in orgasm and came all over the shaft. Truly, it was a stimulating display. Then, tenderly, gingerly, she took herself off the thing and I could hear her sex slurping shut softly, speaking that mysterious word of woman's satisfaction. That woman, I say, will be with child this year. Let me ask you, ladies, can a prick of stone eject the vital semen? Is this how Hercules the God-man was born?

"Oh, god, O O O. . . ."

Better products for happier living. Relax-a-Finger. Underwriter's Laboratory Approved, PATENT PENDING

22

A tall Athenian stood up. Her face was long and horsey and her bones large and strong, but there was a fineness in her features that was lovely and her mound of Venus bulged most voluptuously. Ladies, she said, I don't know about sitting on the prick of Priapos, but I do know about the wonderful leather tools that the sandal makers of this city once made for us. I still have one of these rare appendages and I shall now pass it around, so you may all sample its handsome form.

"Want to try another party?" asked Jim.

"Anything's better than this," said Ellen, hoping for an encounter with that fateful love affair that kept eluding her. It could be tonight, a new party, just a few people.

"Come on," said her red-eyed, totally-smashed friend, "I'll introduce you to . . . to I forget his fucking name, but he's rich."

They walked across the room. Smiling at them near the door was a grey-haired man, who took Ellen's hand and gave her a slight bow, very charming, in the old school way. "Hello," he said. His hair was wavy silver, his eyes baby blue, and his smile grew radiant.

It was snowing, the street was slippery, and the grey-haired gentleman gave Ellen his arm. Slightly loaded herself, she dreamed of possibilities.

The cab finally came, and the three of them climbed in, off to new drinks, new lights, an address on Madison Avenue, a very good address.

"I'm in among the art galleries," said the grey-haired man to Ellen. "Art is my business."

"Are you an artist?"

"A dealer."

So he *is* rich, thought Ellen, and the possibilities began multiplying, a play of lights and digits clicking in her head silently and brightly, like those of a handy pocket-size electronic calculator.

While the Athenian women talked and laughed, one of the serving boys slipped away and walked through the night to the chamber of the Chief Athenian Priest, who was awaiting him.

"We're all such strangers in this city," said the

grey-haired man. "But we'll get to know each other better, won't we?" he added, somewhat mysteriously, thought Ellen, but she liked it, and her little calculator began programming trips to Europe for the purchase of masterpieces and to exotic lands for curios. Life in the arts, click, click, click.

Ellen, Jim, and the distinguished gentleman, who now introduced himself as Gary Neederman, got out of the cab and Ellen wished that Jim would see the impossible triangle he was creating. Well, she thought, he'll probably leave after a drink or two.

The serving boy helped the Chief Priest into his special vestment. All trace of the priest disappeared except his feet, which stuck out at bottom. The rest of him was completely covered by a huge facsimile of the male sexual organ, which now turned in the chamber, went out the door, and walked down a street lined with cheering women of the lower classes, who threw night-blooming flowers before the great walking prick. Its one eye was cast up to heaven, for it looked only to the gods, and never to the trivial affairs of men. The priest, therefore, had to be led by his serving-boy through the street. The boy walked with one arm around the great prick, directing the footsteps of the priest back to the temple of the Athenian women.

And then she was in the most incredible apartment she'd ever seen, anywhere—filled with statues, paintings, exquisite bric-a-brac, all of it set amongst furniture that had come from all over the world, from a long time ago.

From beneath her gown, the Athenian beauty removed

a long leather penis, stuffed with some firm material and sewed with careful stitches. The ladies took it, passing it from hand to hand and giggling, some of them even rubbing it against their sexual parts.

Gary Neederman opened what had once been a medieval altar, of beautifully carved wood, Within it was a complete bar. He gave Ellen a drink and then called to Jim, who was looking at a head of stone, of a beautiful woman, with eyes of stone, staring across the ages.

"Do you like that piece?" asked Gary.

"She knocks me out," said Jim.

Gary handed him a drink. "She's called Demeter. The Greek goddess of marriage and fertility." He turned to Ellen. "Do you believe in the gods?"

"Oh, absolutely," said Ellen, becoming her most charming light-hearted self, as she floated from one superb art object to another.

"I'm afraid," said Gary, "my place is something of a hodge-podge. It's because I'm always buying—and selling, too, of course."

"It's marvelous," said Ellen, going over to him, getting sincerely friendly, getting deep, looking into Gary's lovely baby-blue eyes. "Your taste is perfect."

He lowered his eyes modestly, staring down, she thought, at her shoes, the new Capezios, she was so happy she'd worn them! And his eyes came slowly back up along her legs, and slowly over her thighs, returning again, renewed, to her eyes. "I'm glad you could come, Ellen," he said softly.

"Hey, what the hell is *this*?" asked Jim.

Ellen wanted to hit him with it, whatever it was, and she couldn't really tell, some kind of long leather thing.

The Athenian woman called Lysistrata took the leather penis in her hand, and sighing, said, These used to be manufactured by the Milesian women, but there isn't one to be seen these days anywhere.

"I don't know if it's the real McCoy," said Gary. "I bought it in an alley in Greece. It's supposed to be an early dildo." He turned to Ellen. "If you'll forgive my saying so."

Now it was Ellen's turn to lower her eyes, though she wasn't really the shy type, but Gary seemed so gentle, so refined.

"A dildo? No kidding," said Jim, laying it back down on the table somewhat uneasily.

"I've toyed with the idea of putting together a pornographic collection," said Gary. "I've seen some beautiful pieces." Again he looked significantly at Ellen, and she didn't lower her eyes this time.

"Well," said Jim, knocking down the last of his drink, "I might as well get the hell on home."

"Please," said Gary, with genuine warmth in his voice, "don't go, Jim."

Ellen, though she wanted Jim gone, could not help but be touched by Gary's friendliness, his tact in not wanting Jim to feel pushed away.

"Come on, Jim," said Gary, "drink up. We're in this thing together, aren't we?"

"Alright, one more," said Jim. "I would like to look around at your stuff a little longer."

"Please do, Jim, make yourself completely at home. Ellen, will you excuse me for just a moment? I'd like to get out of this—" He loosened his tie and waited for her assent which she quickly gave with a warm smile.

Now, said the Chief Priest, when he had reached the steps of Demeter's temple, we will celebrate the Great Mystery.

Gary left the room, going through a large door which was faced with oriental lattice-work, through which another room could be seen, dimly lit by a soft red light. Ellen stared for a moment, but Gary was out of sight, somewhere beyond the soft red glow. She joined Jim in front of a pearl cornucopia, out of which gems of all kinds were pouring, and she was sure they were real.

"Quite a pad," said Jim. "You might wake up in the middle of the night screaming, but it's still quite a pad."

Ellen noticed movement through the lattice-work and saw Gary's figure there, indistinguishable, and hesitating just a moment. He's so tall, thought Ellen, and so handsome, and she closed her eyes and realized that she really couldn't remember what he looked like at all, but the impression was there, of something rare, with great natural dignity, with . . .

The priest's voice was muffled, but all the women who had followed him to the temple knew that now he would penetrate the three layers of Mother Earth.

Gary pushed open the lattice-work door and entered naked, except for a huge tail of peacock feathers, which were fastened in his asshole with a cork.

"Kick the pretty peacock!" he cried, skipping into the room, his feathers waving. "Kick the pretty peacock!"

He danced around them, bent over, so that his tail-feathers swayed in the air. "Kick the pretty peacock! Kick the pretty peacock!"

Ellen stood stupified, Jim alongside her. She stared at the gold-encrusted cork which held all the feathers together and which seemed to be wedged far up the art dealer's anus. *"Kick the pretty peacock!"* he hissed, spinning around to face them.

"I don't want to kick you, man," said Jim. He set his drink down and started for the door. The peacock jumped in front of him, wiggling his tail. "Don't be afraid," he said, blocking the door. "Kick the pretty peacock!"

Jim hesitated a moment, looking around for another doorway, and found none. The peacock was blocking the only exit.

"KICK THE PRETTY PEACOCK! KICK THE PRETTY PEACOCK!"

Jim brought his foot back and sent the end of his shoe into the peacock's tail feathers. The glorious bird fell forward, stumbling onto his knees. "Take something from this room!" he cried. "Take anything you want and then go."

Jim looked around quickly, grabbed Demeter's stone head, and pushed past the peacock, whose wildly painted eyes were smiling.

He walked through the front door of the temple, through red drapes that represented the Magnificent

Labia; he walked through the center portion of the temple, designated as the Grand Hall of the Vagina; and finally he came to the back of the temple at the door of the Great Uterus, where he prayed.

"Kick the pretty peacock!"

"Wait for me, Jim!" cried Ellen, but the peacock was in her way now, shaking and rocking his thousand-eyed tail.

"Kick the pretty peacock and then take something from his room. Take anything you like."

Ellen raised her square-toed Capezio and send a hard fast shot into the peacock's tail, which caught him off balance and sent him sprawling to the floor. She grabbed the ancient leather dildo and ran past the peacock, who lay on the floor in his feathers, shooting semen into the air.

On the other side of the door, in the room of the Great Uterus itself, the noble Athenian women continued telling their obscene stories, while the Chief Priest prayed for good crops, intelligent children, and venereal disease to be visited upon his country's enemies.

23

"Ah, ha! So I caught you, Edwina, playing with yourself in the bathroom again."

"Please, Mommy, please don't hit me."

"Playing with yourself. Sticking your finger into yourself, aren't you. Let me smell it. Yes, you are. Why, you're going to get a good crack for this."

"Please, Mommy, don't hit me."

"What a disgusting child you are. Everytime I peek in the keyhole at you, I find you playing with your foofy. I never played with my foofy. It's a filthy disgusting sickening dirty habit. Don't you know it can make you cross-eyed?"

"Oh, Mommy!"

Well, ladies of Athens, I raise my cup again, and drain it of wine, feeling myself to be getting quite drunk, and . . . but what is this I see on the bottom of the glass? What a charming picture! Do you see, my dears, it is a glass on which is depicted the love struggle of a man and woman.

"You aren't letting any of the little boys touch you, are you, Edwina?"

"No, Mommy."

"You must never let a little boy touch you. And if he asks you to take down your panties and show him your foofy, you call a policeman. Do you understand? Little boys like that should be locked up. They should be burnt at the stake."

"Yes, Mommy."

"Now come along and get into your pajamas. And see that you don't have any nightmares again tonight. I'm not getting my necessary eight hours' sleep with the way you're carrying on these nights."

Her legs are up around his, and she has pulled him into her. How nice it is to drink from a cup decorated with such lovely art. I have a similar set of bowls at home for my children. The bottoms are painted with delightful scenes of copulation in all forms—young ladies being stuck in all positions by their lovers. My children enjoy their cereal more that way. It occupies their minds as they are eating. All the women on my block are using them now. The children enjoy it so.

"All right, here's a little treat for you, some nice hot milk with crackers in your Bugs Bunny bowl. See Elmer Fudd in there chasing Bugs with a shotgun? Isn't that nice? You drink your milk and Bugs and Elmer will be in your dreams."

"Yes, Mommy."

"Goodnight, Edwina. And remember. . . ."

"Yes, Mommy?"

"Foofy will drive you insane."

24

Sir Filbert Morley, the eminent doctor of the antique Greek language, is burning the candle to a stub, and the expression on his face is pained as he reads to himself from an early Greek text he is attempting to translate. The lusty god Bacchus speaks: *"Yes, yes, they knew this, how to f... in the teeth of the rower beneath."*

Face reddening, Sir Filbert raises his eyes from the ancient work. Even in his mind, he cannot bring himself to utter the vulgarity he has found in the great work.

". . . dash it all, this just can't be. . . ."

And he makes some scribblings in his notebook, then crosses them out and scribbles some more, still mumbling to himself.

"Sophocles simply did not say this. He was too fine a poet. . . ."

Sir Filbert works in a fever. The housekeeper looks in and brings him his evening milk. She has watched over him faithfully for years, while he has slaved over the ancient tongue of the Greeks.

"Hard at it, sir?" she says, clearing a little space for his milk glass.

". . . simply couldn't mean this. . . ." The great scholar barely notices the good woman, and so she leaves him, backing away to the doorway from where she watches him in his feverish work.

"Dash it all!" Sir Filbert's notebooks are opened to the final pages of The Frogs. *Dash it all, I've nearly got through the thing, but this line here about emitting gaseous vapour in the teeth of the rower beneath—it simply won't do, old boy. The Queen would be outraged by such a line and I might be pitched out of Oxford.*

"Will there be anything else, Sir Filbert?"

"The Greeks, Mrs. Ficky, were a noble people."

"Indeed, sir."

"Their art the highest, their poetry the most sublime."

"Oh, yes, quite, sir, so I've heard."

"I believe, Mrs. Ficky, that I am dealing here with a spurious copy of an ancient work, a work of magnificence that has been besmirched by the hand of a vulgar person who has dared to tamper with the lines of the noble poet Sophocles."

"Oh, no, sir!"

"Yes, Mrs. Ficky! There is a line in this play that cannot be attributed to the great genius we know as Sophocles. Some vile jester, some impudent scoundrel somewhere in the ages, has seen fit to stick his own corrupt mind into the great work of art we call The Frogs."

"Would you like some more milk, sir?"

"No, Mrs. Ficky, thank you, that will be all. I see the solution clearly before me now."

"That's good, sir. Well, good night then, sir."

It's obvious what Sophocles meant in this instance. Clear as the nose on my face. He meant to say "*blow one's nose in the teeth of the rower below.*" That is definitely it. Blow one's nose. It has a kind of ring to it, I should say. Yes, that's it. The work may now go before the public. Victoria will approve.

25

Ladies of Athens, said the next speaker, I know that just the mention of her name will make you sigh. I am speaking of Phryne, the beautiful harlot. You all remember her; the artist Praxiteles employed her as a model for the magnificent gold statue which today stands so gloriously in the temple of Apollo at Delphi.

She was, perhaps, the most lovely woman of her time, judging from the sublime proportions of her statue. And she had the habit of always clothing herself in the most modest attire. Never was she seen in public, as we are tonight, in such brief and provocative costume. Always she was wrapped demurely in her white robe, and in this way incited men to lust for her that they might know the treasures that hid beneath her gown.

Alas, she was too beautiful and too popular. Certain jealous wives of prominent politicians started up a storm against the gorgeous girl, claiming that she was corrupting the youth of Athens.

"Oh, my god, Jeffrey, look at this magazine I just picked up at the drugstore! Isn't that our little Edwina there, posing naked amongst some kind of tropical vegetation?"

"Why, let me see, Penelope. Let me see that-there magazine. So it is. Begosh, you're right. It is Edwina posing naked amongst some greenery. By the Lord Jesus, she's got a pair of dugs on her, doesn't she?"

"Jeffrey!"

"I was just commentin'."

"What will the neighbors say? We may be asked to move our modular home out of Gladiola Drive."

"The hell you say! Our modular home?"

"They've been against us from the first, the people in all their fancy houses. If they see this-here picture of our daughter all naked, we're sure to be the cause of a public meeting."

"I'd better get my coat on."

"Yes, Jeffrey, you'd better go straight to the drugstore and buy up every copy of this magazine you see."

"I'm on my way, Penelope."

Well, ladies of Athens, strange as it may seem, the

beautiful prostitute was actually brought to court for practicing her art. That shows you just how low a country can get when it has nothing better to do than to run its prostitutes into the courts of law.

"I'll take these here three copies of *Rear End* magazine, please."

Ladies of Athens, you can imagine how the courtroom was—packed with people. Everyone who had ever seen the beautiful Phryne was there—all her old lovers and so many admirers from afar that they were lined up into the streets. Trying a prostitute in a court of law was, of course, an unprecedented affair bound to cause much public interest. For after all, what law had she broken?

"Hello, Edwina, this is your mother, calling long distance. Are you there . . . is there something wrong with this connection? Hello, Edwina, what's going on—are you having some kind of party? I can't hear you very well. What are there, drug fiends all around I imagine . . . hello, Edwina, don't you dare speak to me that way. Listen, young lady, I have in front of me right at this very moment a copy of *Rear End* magazine and it is open to page twenty-two. So there! What am I talking about? I'll tell you what I'm talking about. I'm talking about your naked body, totally exposed for everyone on Gladiola Drive to see. You've wrecked your modular home, do you know that? We're ruined."

Ladies of Athens, the prosecution spoke unheard-of accusations against beautiful Phryne, calling her a disgrace to the nation, and a threat to the well-being of its children. The prosecutor made the noble art of prostitution sound like something bad, can you believe that? But such was the power of his oration that many in the court were swayed and harsh glances were being thrown at Phryne, who sat demurely as ever upon a bench in front of all, wrapped as always in her modest gown.

"Edwina, how could you do such a thing to us? Tell me—tell your mother—how could you do such a thing as take your clothes off? Did you get paid for it? How much did you get? Is that all? For a lousy twenty-five dollars, you've practically killed your father. Yes, he's at the drugstore now."

When the prosecution had spoken its case against Phryne, ladies of Athens, it looked grim indeed. We'd never thought before about our prostitutes in any way but as happy girls who made others happy. Now we'd heard described in detail just how vicious they were, and how the appearance of such a one as this Phryne in our city had caused mental degeneracy among our babies, our children, our sons.

"Edwina, tell me truthfully, I have to know—I raised you from a baby—are there any other photographs like these of you around. There are? All right, wait till I get a pencil, just a minute, you tell me where I can get them, I've got to get them immediately, before the antimodular-home committee has its next meeting. They're just waiting for something like this, you know. They claim our modular home has lowered the value of their properties. Just think what they'll do with your body, laying naked there in the vegetables. All right now, where else have you . . . where? How many times? Oh, my god. Edwina, I'm having one of my attacks, you've given it to me, my head is pounding. Hundreds of times, Edwina, you've done it hundreds of times. Oh, my god."

"Hello, Pen, I'm home with three *Rear Ends,* bought every last copy they had . . . oh, you're on the phone."

"Your father just came in, Edwina. He's sick all over about this. He looks terrible; his heart is broken."

But the defense was not to be so easily beaten, ladies of Athens. Phryne's counsel was the wise Hyperides. He knew the mood of the courtroom and saw that the judges were ready to condemn the prostitute to some severe punishment. Hyperides did not waste words. He bid Phryne to stand and come to him at the center of the courtroom. She did. And then all of Athens saw that which it had never seen before in public. The lawyer asked her to remove her gown.

Oh, ladies of Athens, as she slowly undid the clasps you could have heard a pin drop. Every breath was drawn, and then her bodice fell open and there were her beautiful breasts, so pure, so perfectly formed, and then her stomach, like a ball of golden butter, and then down went her gown to the floor, and she was revealed entirely, including her magnificent mount of Aphrodite. The courtroom gasped, so splendid was she. The wise counsel for defense made her slowly turn around, so that she was revealed from behind as well.

Already, ladies of Athens, the judges were smiling. But Phryne did not smile. She looked as modest as the youngest of the goddesses, and was this the creature accused of corrupting youth? Then let it be so corrupted as to know loveliness like this!

The judges, certain that here was the incarnation of Aphrodite herself, did not dare to bring a case against her. The accusations were dismissed. Phryne slowly dressed herself, amidst cheers from the courtroom. Fearing any further such displays, the judges that day made it law that no such disrobing must ever take place in a court of law again. But, of course, ladies of Athens, it isn't likely that any prostitute will ever be dragged into the temple of justice again, for all saw that day how innocent these women are.

"Edwina, how could you expose your body this way, after all the wonderful college education we gave you, which you've thrown up in our faces . . . Edwina . . . Edwina? She hung up. Jeffrey! Stop ogling that magazine and listen to me!"

26

Help me out of this confounded prick suit, dear boy, said the priest.

His assistant helped him out of the great organ and the priest went through the last door of Demeter's temple, into the deepest chamber of the sacred building, where the distinguished ladies of Athens were gathered, lying about in various states of undress.

"Fred, are you sure this is a Broadway show? It looks awful dingy in here."

"Ethel, haven't you been married to me for forty years?

When I said a Broadway show I meant a Broadway show."

"But, Fred, what were all those magazine racks in the room we just came through with pictures of naked men and women on them?"

"Those were programs, Ethel."

"My God, Fred, what kind of show is this?"

"It's the new wave in drama," said Fred. "It's filled with social commentary."

"It's terribly smoky in here. Is that a stage, Fred? It's so small. And they sure don't have many seats in here for a Broadway theater. It's more like a back room."

"It's a new concept, Ethel, entirely new. Intimate theater."

"Fred, I—"

The lights dimmed suddenly and the curtains parted. Onto the stage walked a tall beautiful black girl, dressed in a red garter belt and panties, and a black bra with red hands painted on it. "Man," said the actress, "I sure am hungry."

"Fred, this isn't a Broadway play!"

"For heaven's sake, Ethel, if you'll take time to read it the sign outside says Broadway and Forty-second Street. Now just relax and enjoy the show."

"Sure like to get something to *eat,*" said the black actress, casually removing her stockings, and gracefully extending her long black legs.

There was a knock on the door of the stage set, which wobbled back and forth precariously.

"Yeah, come on in," said the black girl.

"Did you order a pizza pie?" asked a young blond-haired man, dressed in a white delivery-boy's suit.

"I sure did, honey, bring it on and lay it down where I can look at it."

"That will be two dollars and fifty cents," said the delivery boy.

"Honey," said the black girl, walking slowly over to the delivery boy, "I ain't got but a dollar. What can I give you in exchange for this pie?" The black girl reached behind her and opened her bra, so that it fell open and off of her, revealing her two large breasts, with their faint red nipples hard and pouting in the spotlight.

"Fred! This is—"

"Shut up, Ethel, and eat your popcorn."

"Just take a feel on me," said the black girl.

The delivery boy began to play shyly with her breasts.

"Fred, I am a member of the Scranton, Pennsylvania PTA and so are you!"

The black girl unbuttoned the delivery-boy's trousers, and the young man was soon standing with his pants off, a long graceful penis hanging between his legs.

A whisper caught in Ethel's throat as she decided that it might be better to pay more close attention to the play, so she could give a full report on it at the next Parent-Teachers' Association meeting. She focused on the delivery-boy's penis and took mental notes.

"Honey," said the black girl, "you can't fuck nobody with that dick. You better let me suck on it a while."

They will never believe me back in Scranton. I wish I'd brought my little Brownie camera.

"You gettin' a little harder now, honey."

When the delivery-boy's member was completely engorged, the black girl removed her panties and garter belt and laid herself down on a mattress on the stage floor. The delivery boy crawled onto her.

The High Priestess sighed when the priest, after a moment's fumbling, inserted his member into the sacrificial hole, so hot and wet, and the ladies of Athens watched wistfully. The year would be fertile, the crops would prosper, and many young sons would be born to the nation.

Suddenly the lights went up in the middle of the action. A man in a police uniform stepped onto the stage. "All right, folks, the show's over. This place has no proper ventilation and is in violation of several other public ordinances."

"Shit, honey," said the black girl, sliding out from under the delivery boy. "Just when we were gettin' to the good part."

The delivery-boy's member was still high in the air.

"Put that away, buster," said the police officer.

"I can't," said the delivery boy. "I'm a Method actor."

"POLICE HARASSMENT!" shouted a voice from the audience.

"COITUS INTERRUPTUS!"

"YEAH, FUCK OFF, FLATFOOT! GO AND ARREST THE MOTHERFUCKER WHO ROBBED MY PAD LAST NIGHT!"

"Fred, what's going to happen to us? Are we under arrest?"

Our sacrifice is so thrilling this year, said the High Priestess, as the priest shot into her, groaning and heaving his testicles. The land would truly be blessed by the gods.

"All right, folks, this way out. Let's not have any trouble. Your money will be refunded at the door."

"Fred, you are not going to buy any of those magazines!"

"Of course not, Ethel, I'm just looking for a souvenir of New York."

The High Priestess rose from her couch, wiping the love potion from her thighs where it ran white and warm. Well, ladies, we've told stories to please Demeter, said the priestess, and we have performed the sacred ritual intercourse. Now let us dance, all of us. Dance, ladies of Athens, and remember Pasiphae, who was married to a king, but was in love with a bull.

"YOU MUST FEEL GUILT OVER THIS!" shouted Father.

"What is it, Father?" asked the trembling daughter.

"Mother has reported to me the finding of spermazooti in your handkerchief."

Pasiphae was walking in the moonlight, when suddenly she was taken by the sight of the great member and massive testicles of the pastured bull.

"Do you have any whoopie cushions? I'd like one for my lodge."

"Spermazoota, that is what I said and that is what I mean!"

"Daddy, it's just mucus. I have a head cold."

"Martha, bring the strap. This young lady needs her

panties rolled down and a few lessons drilled on her hinder."

"I ain't got any whoopie cushions in stock at the moment, sir. But I got an air-raid siren you can attach to a toilet seat. Goes off when you put the seat down."

"Sounds good. Let me have one."

"Fred!"

"Ethel, it's just for the Lodge's Annual Underprivileged Children's Picnic. It'll give the kids a laugh."

The bull lowered his head, came closer to Pasiphae, who was enchanted by the tremendous penis which had unsheathed itself and hung out now, wet and glistening in the moonlight, larger than a man's arm.

"Now repeat after me, young lady, *I will have nothing more to do with spermazootz.*"

"Hit her some more with the strap, Axel."

"I think I will, Martha, thank you."

Pasiphae went closer to the bull, drawn irresistibly by the great black shining organ. She reached out and gently touched it.

"There's too many fuckin' animals in this book, kid," said Mr. Pant. "I can't use it."

SUNRISE